The Spider's Web
A Novella and Other Stories

Also by Wayne Greenhaw

Alabama: A State of Mind, Community Communications and the Business Council of Alabama, 2000
Alabama on My Mind: A Collection, Sycamore Press, 1986*
Alabama: Portrait of a State, Black Belt Press, 1998
Elephants in the Cottonfields: Ronald Reagan and the New Republican South, Macmillan, 1981
Flying High: Inside Big-Time Drug Smuggling, Dodd Mead, 1984
The Making of a Hero: Lt. William L. Calley and the My Lai Massacre, Touchstone, 1971
Montgomery: Center Stage in the South, Windsor Publications, 1990
Montgomery: The Biography of a City, The Advertiser Company, 1993
Montgomery: The River City, River City Publishing, 2002*
My Heart Is in the Earth: True Stories of Alabama and Mexico, River City Publishing, 2001*
Watch Out for George Wallace, Prentice-Hall, 1976

NOVELS
Beyond the Night, Black Belt Press, 1999*
The Golfer, J. B. Lippincott, 1968, also Sycamore Press, 1991*
Hard Travelin', Touchstone, 1971
King of Country, Black Belt Press, 1994*
The Long Journey, River City Publishing, 2002*

DRAMA
Rose: A Southern Lady, a one-actress play
The Spirit Tree, a play in two acts

SHORT STORIES
Tombigbee and Other Stories, Sycamore Press, 1991*

Titles marked with an asterisk (*) are available from River City Publishing. Phone toll-free 1 (877) 408-7078, or phone 265-6753 local, or order via e-mail at our Web site, www.rivercitypublishing.com.

The Spider's Web

A Novella and Other Stories
By Wayne Greenhaw

RIVER CITY
PUBLISHING
Montgomery, Alabama

Published in the United States by River City Publishing,
1719 Mulberry St., Montgomery, AL 36106

Printed in the United States
Designed by Lissa Monroe

First Edition

Library of Congress Cataloging-in-Publication Data:

For Carolyn and Al Newman
with great affection

"Life is beautiful.
Life is sad."
— Vladimir Nabokov

One

Looking back in time, I see a boy standing on the edge of a pier, casting a long and crooked image onto the surface of mirror-slick water of the lake.

Behind him, the man ordered, "Stand straight."

"I'm standing straight," the boy said.

The man, his scoutmaster, pressed cold hands against the sun-tanned skin of the boy's back. As the man touched, he made a sound deep in his throat and caused the boy to wonder.

"What's wrong?" the fourteen-year-old asked, his body stiffening.

After the man's fingers traced the spinal column from the boy's neck to the top of his swimming trunks, the man said, "Your backbone's crooked."

The boy's brain raced like a runaway car, as if he knew at that moment his entire life would change, as if his world would be tumbling in an out-of-control spiral that would end in some fiery emotional catastrophe, like a car-truck-motorcycle crash would affect the lives of the people from the moment of impact to the end of their lives.

I know what the boy thought because I am the boy, Thomas Morgan Reed. A child of Depression-punished parents, a mother born and raised in poverty, traveling the South with her mother and father in a wagon pulled by a pair of mules, being moved from place to place, school to school, reading every book she could get her hands on, reading Herman Melville and Jane

Austen in English and Victor Hugo in French. She never knew a real home until she met my father, who was born in a small town in north Alabama and lived most of his life there. Daddy's parents were not poor, like hers. Neither were they rich. They had a nice house, a small farm, and his father worked for the county's largest cotton planter when the crop was planted, tended, and harvested. To escape small-town boredom, Daddy became a traveling salesman, yearning constantly for a new territory, a richer commission, more customers, people to listen to and talk with.

Mama came out of the Depression tough, strong, smart, and determined never to be poor again. Daddy decided that never again would he, like his father, a Presbyterian Scot, squeeze the life out of every dime that ever crossed his palm. Daddy was damned if he'd let money rule his life. Daddy made a dollar to spend and enjoy. He bought a brand new car every year. He explained it, saying he needed it for his business. "When you put as many miles as I do on a car, they wear out fast," he told Mama. "Besides, out there on the road people respect you when you're driving a spiffy set of wheels." When he slid onto the seat of a new Chevy, clamped his hands on a slick, new steering wheel, whiffed the fresh upholstery, rubbed his fingers across the shiny dashboard, his face broke out in a smile big enough to win any cynic's heart, even Mama's.

While Daddy sought solace on the road, Mama was anchored to the home, like it was a buoy to keep us all afloat.

"I'll tell your parents about this problem," Aaron Brainlevel, the scoutmaster, said.

When I turned and stared up into his face, the sun glaring into my eyes, I squinted and moved into his shadow.

"What do you think it is?" I asked, trying to read the depth of seriousness in his somber expression. He liked to think of himself as a drill sergeant, a teacher of immature bodies and minds, molding them into the shape he desired as a cracker-jack leader. He was a man who tried to carry himself high above the crowd. He seldom cracked a joke or let out a belly-laugh. When the other camp trainers joked about their wives and girlfriends, Aaron Brainlevel glared at them with sullen disregard, even disgust.

"I don't know exactly what it is," Aaron Brainlevel said. "But I do know it's interfering with your natural growth pattern, the way you're twisted to one side, the way your left shoulder droops, like you're holding a heavy weight in your left hand, pulling you down."

For a moment his seriousness sent a chill over my body. Then I flexed my knees, lowered my head, and dove into the still, dark lake water.

When I came up he was standing at the edge of the pier. "I don't think you should be diving, Thomas. It might hurt something."

I shook my head, slinging the water from my hair. "I've been diving all my life," I said. "Since I was a little boy," I added. "I know how to dive, just like I know how to swim."

"But you didn't know your back was crooked then," he said.

I kicked my feet, paddled my hands, treading water.

I threw my arm over my head, cupping the water, bringing my arm back, kicking my feet up and down, up and down. If I wanted, I could swim to China. I swam a hundred feet out from the pier, made my turn, and swam back.

As soon as my hand touched the wooden ladder, Aaron Brainlevel said, "Thomas, you better come out of the water."

I played like I didn't hear him, threw my head back, closed my eyes and tried not to breath through my nose as I did a dozen backstrokes.

When I sucked water up my nose, I was forced to stop, cough, and change my direction.

When I did, Mr. Brainlevel screamed, "Thomas! Listen to me now!"

I swam easily and effortlessly to the ladder. I slung the water from my hair and looked up into his anxiety-riddled face. "What's wrong, Mr. Brainlevel?"

"Come out of the water now, son," he said.

I started to tell him I was not his son, but I bit my tongue, pulled up the ladder, and took the towel from his hands.

When I got home from camp I did not tell Mama and Daddy about my back, but they learned several days later when Mr. Brainlevel called. Mama stared into my face and asked why I didn't tell them. I dropped my chin and shrugged. "I don't know."

"Well," she said, "it sounds very serious. Come over here."

I shuffled to her and she put her hands on my upper arms. She lifted my left shoulder. "Hold it up," she said, frowning.

I squared my shoulders.

"Stand straight," she said.

"I am," I said.

"You're slouching," she said.

I was standing as straight as I could, but when I looked at myself in Mama's floor-to-ceiling mirror, I stared at a boy who leaned to the left. The Kodak photos that Mama had taken of me and my Scout friends when she and Daddy visited camp on Sunday afternoon showed my skinny legs sticking from my swimming trunks, my arms hanging at my sides, and my left shoulder several inches lower than the right.

Looking at myself through eyes colored by Mr. Brainlevel's diagnosis made me know that something was terribly wrong. I heard Mama and Daddy talking into the night. I lay in bed and stared up into the shadows drifting across the ceiling.

Mama took me to see our family doctor, who said there was no doubting the situation but he didn't do the intricate and complex kind of work that it would take to straighten my back.

A week after I started the ninth grade we visited an orthopedic surgeon who had experience with curvatures of the spine.

T w o

"You have scoliosis," the doctor stated. "Curvature of the spine results from a birth defect or a light case of polio when you were a baby."

Mama frowned. She didn't remember my suffering from polio. I wondered how she could not remember something so significant. I didn't remember being sick with polio. Weren't you supposed to be crippled if you had such a disease? In 1954, it was about the worst thing a person could have.

I shivered, thinking about the word and its meaning. Mama had warned against swimming in a pool with hundreds of other kids. If one had polio, she said, my brother or I might catch the disease. Still, we went to Queen City pool in the summers whenever we got the chance—when Mama or one of the other mothers could take us. Mama warned, "Swim away from the other children. And if a child starts coughing, get out of the water immediately." Whenever a swimmer came up coughing, spitting water, Donnie Lee and I made for the ladder, wrapped towels around our shoulders, and waited for the cough to end.

Thinking about the occasion of my childhood illness, Mama nodded and said, "He had a fever when he was several weeks old. We had to take him back to the hospital. He was put into an incubator for a week or ten days."

The doctor nodded solemnly.

I pulled my shirt around my body and began buttoning, listening to them discuss my medical history. A knot hardened inside my sternum as I thought on something terrible happening when I was too young to remember, something too horrible even to imagine. It had happened without my knowing, then it stayed hidden inside, embedded in the far corner of my being, void of color or movement, waiting dormant to be extracted and examined. Now it was brought into the light of day and was sitting on the table to be analyzed, like my naked skin that had been poked and prodded and examined by this chubby, baldheaded, bespectacled man who was suddenly an integral and important part of my life.

"The entire procedure will mean a year out of Thomas's life," Dr. Albert Braswell said. His words stunned me: a year gone, like that, passionless, clinical words from the mouth of a middle-aged man who'd first gazed upon me less than thirty minutes ago. And now he was extracting a year from my life.

He began explaining the procedure: how I would be hospitalized at the children's clinic in Birmingham, fifty miles away from home, placed in a body cast, which would be twisted and maneuvered to straighten my spinal column; then he would perform a series of surgeries, weaving live bone through my vertebrae, which would fuse together, strengthening the shaft, making my back stiff forever. It would be a long, drawn-out procedure. When he finished with me, I'd be fifteen: old enough to drive a car but without the ability to stand on my own.

Next summer I should be a sophomore in high school. But what will happen if I miss all that time from school? Will they put me back a grade? They couldn't, I thought. They can't! All of my friends will be in the tenth grade next year, playing football or in the band or . . .

"You won't be able to play football ever again," he said in his dry tone as though reading my mind.

I glared into his round face, his colorless lips that moved and made sounds.

"The best exercise will be swimming," he said. "You will need to swim every day. But no diving. If you dive into the water, it could damage your spine. It could cause irreversible damage."

As he spoke, tears came to my mother's eyes. She tried to turn and blink them away, but she couldn't. I reached out and took her trembling hand. I held it. I thought about John Wayne or Lash LaRue or Hopalong Cassidy, my boyhood heroes, and thought what they would do in such a predicament. I squeezed Mama's fingers. She blinked again. Then she pulled her fingers from mine and dug into her purse.

Dr. Braswell did not hand her the box of Kleenex on the stainless steel shelf next to him. He continued talking, "Much of your recuperation following the operations can take place at home," while she blew her nose and took my hand again and squeezed it.

"How long?" Mama asked.

"He'll be in the hospital at least a month before the first surgery. The operations will be performed about two weeks apart. Then he will remain in the hospital for another two or three weeks to make sure he has no complications. Then he can be transported home to Tuscaloosa in an ambulance. After another six weeks to two months we will put him in a short, waist-length cast over one shoulder. He will need to wear the short cast another six weeks to two months." His words, quick and flat, swept through me like a fever. I felt like crying, but I didn't. It had nothing to do with courage. It had to do with fright. And I didn't want to scare Mama more than she already was.

When we got home, Mama told Daddy, "He didn't even cry. I bawled like a baby, but Thomas just sat there and held my hand. He was so brave." I felt proud. I didn't tell her that I didn't cry because I was numb. My entire body had numbed with the sound of the doctor's words. I didn't cry because I couldn't think—and couldn't feel. For a change, I had done the right thing to please her.

I did not always succeed in pleasing my parents. When I made an F in English in the fourth grade because I refused to memorize a dumb poem, my mother cried and my father got so flustered that he grew red in the face, threw up his hands, and stormed out of the house. He rode away in his new Chevrolet and didn't come home for three days, gone, he said, out on the road where he called on customers, calling Mama at night to see how things were progressing back home. It was the way Daddy did things; he escaped into his own world, far removed from the everyday life we knew on Magnolia Avenue in the heart of the suburbs on the eastern edge of Tuscaloosa. I had barricaded myself in my room, shutting the door and burrowing my face into my pillow and crying profusely, my body shivering with fright, thinking that I had personally destroyed what family I had. Whatever happened, it was my fault.

T h r e e

Everything happened so fast. I was in school one day and on my way to the hospital the next. I had talked with my best friend Jake and told him I'd write while I was away. He said he would too. He said he would visit the hospital, but I saw the unsure look in his eyes. Neither of us had ever had a friend who had to be hospitalized, other than an overnight stay for an appendectomy or something. Jake didn't offer any free advice. He was unusually quiet.

Daddy drove fast. The pine-dotted hardwood forest hugged the sides of the two-lane blacktop. Daddy lighted a new Kool cigarette off the butt of the one he'd been smoking. The back seat, where I sat directly behind him close to the door, reeked of familiar smells: after-shave lotions, shampoo, soaps, liquids used by beauty shop operators to color and wave women's hair, and other supplies Daddy sold to beauticians and barbers across Alabama and Mississippi.

"What do you say we stop at Ollie's and have a big, fat barbecue before we go to the hospital?" he said, smiling around the Kool that bobbed between his smoke-spotted lips while he glanced up into the rearview mirror at my image.

I sat sullen amid the smells tainted by an occasional whiff of smoke escaping the corners of his mouth. I stared at his watery eyes in the mirror, not answering.

"What you say, Myrt?" he asked, shifting his glance toward Mama, who'd fastened herself near the front passenger door like it was a buoy to cling to, not saying anything, her jaw taut.

"A tangy Ollie barbecue sound good?" Daddy tried to make his voice sing. At times like these he was an actor playing a part, trying to be convincing, trying to break the barriers of our self-imposed cold bubble, using all the talent of his personality.

I was more like Mama. I had yet to develop my father's persona. I was too fourteen, withdrawn unto myself, seeking an inner satisfaction or a cocoon where I could hide my true feelings.

Daddy reached out the only way he knew.

"Eat a big ol' Ollie's dripping with sauce. It'll be good for your tummy and great for your attitude." He tried to make his voice lilt, like a singer's, but I didn't smile. Mama nibbled at the ends of her fingernails.

Daddy's mouth tightened. "Don't do that, honey," he said. "You've got pretty nails."

Mama regarded her fingers critically. She mumbled something.

"I know a lot of cosmetologists who'd give anything for nails like yours," he said.

"Nails are nails," Mama said.

"Oh, no," Daddy insisted, the gray ashes falling onto the broad chest of his pale yellow nylon wash-and-wear shirt. "Nails can be weak or strong."

"Mine are weak," Mama said.

"They're not big and long and thick. But they're . . ."

"Weak," Mama said.

"They'd be strong, if you'd let 'em."

Mama shifted on the seat, turned and looked at me fully in the face. Her hard look softened. In a compliant voice, she said, "Do you want a barbecue, Thomas?"

I shrugged like only a fourteen-year-old can shrug.

"If you don't want a damn barbecue," Daddy said, "say so." He rolled down his window and flipped the butt of his cigarette into the wind.

"Harold!" Mama said.

Daddy glanced again into the overhead mirror.

"Don't just sit there," he said, "like a cow turd or something."

"Harold!" Mama's voice sharpened.

Rolling the window up hurriedly, he fished into his breast pocket, shook up another cigarette, stuck it between his lips, flicked open his Bic and lighted the end. After he sucked smoke up his nose, he opened his mouth and exhaled a gray cloud.

He said nothing, pushed the Chevrolet faster, and glanced again at my reflection. Eyes mapped with fiery red veins blinked, then clouded.

"You can slow down, Harold," Mama said. "We're not going to a fire," she added her customary warning.

Daddy looked toward her, then back at the road. He stomped the brake, turned the steering wheel abruptly, skidded the tires that squealed against the asphalt, and barely missed a wide-eyed brown deer that leaped full stride, legs extended, and disappeared into the thick woods as suddenly as she had appeared.

"Damn!" Daddy exclaimed, straightening the wheel, pushing us straight down the highway at a faster speed.

After a moment of silence, Daddy said, "Pretty thing, wasn't he?"

"She," I said.

His eyes caught my reflection again.

"She was a doe," I said.

"I didn't get a look at its whang," Daddy said with a smile.

"Harold!" Mama said.

"She didn't have horns," I said.

"Antlers," he said, winking at me when I looked up at the mirror.

I smiled.

After miles of watching the woods and seeing no more deer, after I leaned back and shut my eyes and tried to imagine my life in the hospital, after none of us said a word for minutes, I said, "An Ollie's might be pretty good."

Daddy looked up, clear-eyed, into the mirror. "You ever wonder what it'd be like to've been a cowboy or an outlaw in the old days?" Daddy asked the recurring question that lived always on the edge of his brain. Years ago his question had delighted me, sent electrodes bristling through my brain to stimulate my imagination, evoking sudden scenes of riding in long-coats with the outlaw Rube Burrow, whose daring exploits—robbing trains filled with gold the yankee industrialists had made from Southern coal mines and the iron industry, a wealth of money extracted from the South that was headed north to big cities—had been the subject of many of Daddy's rambling monologues as we rode across the Alabama countryside. The Bankhead Forest between Birmingham and the Tennessee River had been the outlaws' hideout, where they took refuge in deep, dark caves after they handed out their ill-gotten riches to the poor folks in the rural hamlets and farms scattered across northwest Alabama in the 1880s and '90s. However, after my seventh-grade history teacher described Rube Burrow as "just another sorry, crooked thief hunted-down and shot-to-death by sheriff's deputies in Vernon, Alabama, the seat of Lamar County," I never again had romantic, runaway thoughts about a Robin Hood roaming the South in search of yankee gold. After the teacher's remarks, I began thinking all of Daddy's stories were made-up drivel designed to corrupt my young mind.

Now, while Daddy spoke of a fantasy, trying to draw me away from a head filled with sorrow, I sat stiffly on the backseat and stared ahead through the cloud of smoke that crowned his iron-gray hair. I looked toward the highway that had widened and was now bordered by service stations, truck stops, small businesses. We climbed atop a viaduct over a web of railroad tracks, then moved onto the four-lane boulevard that would take us into the heart of Birmingham.

Daddy veered right onto the backstreet to Ollie's, where his old friend made succulent barbecue sandwiches with a mustard-based sauce that gave the meat a sweet-tangy flavor when it was lifted from hickory coals where it had been cooking all night. Part of the thrill of any good barbecue joint was the smell of the meat slowly cooking, the smoke flavoring the air with its aroma, making the customer hungry by the simple act of opening the door and entering.

The thought of it made my stomach eager for a taste.

By the time Daddy pulled into the parking lot I was ready to chomp down on a fresh bun stuffed with pulled brown meat drenched with yellow-tinged liquid.

After Ollie came over and shook Daddy's hand and Daddy told him how I was on my way to the hospital, I sat on my hands and tried not to fidget or look too awkward for a boy who was too skinny and leaned to one side when he tried to stand straight.

Daddy was explaining to the restaurateur what scoliosis was when the waitress brought our sandwiches, each wrapped in wax paper.

As I unwrapped mine and picked it up, sauce ran out the side and dripped onto the front of my plaid shirt.

"Be careful, Son," Mama said, shoving a sheath of napkins toward me.

I leaned forward over the table, opened my mouth, and took a big bite.

Sauce squeezed around the corners of my mouth and ran down my chin before I could lick it up or wipe it off.

"Son!" Mama said.

I said nothing as I wiped my mouth, chewed, swallowed, and took another enormous bite. I washed it down with a swallow of Coke.

Daddy ate as eagerly as I while Mama lifted slivers of meat from the bun with her thumb and forefinger, nibbling daintily.

"That ain't no way to eat barbecue," Daddy said between bites.

Mama threw him a look that he ignored while he licked the corners of his mouth.

I almost laughed but didn't.

When Daddy slid out of the plastic-covered seat he broke wind with a sudden POOP.

"Harold!" Mama exclaimed.

Daddy grinned, said nothing, and strode hastily toward the men's room.

F o u r

The hospital lobby smelled like rubbing alcohol mixed with a strange gaseous substance. I waited while my parents filled out lengthy forms.

After being lifted up into the bowels of the hospital, we were led by a tall, black orderly through metal doors into a large children's ward room.

A thick-shouldered boy in a wheelchair rolled straight up to me, extended a hand covered with so much dark hair it looked like fur, and boomed, "I'm Lanier Thompkins," in a forceful baritone. His head was large with dark-green eyes hooded by bushy, black brows. His unruly hair was black as a raven's wings and stuck out in puffs above his ears.

I introduced myself in a voice no louder than a whisper.

After I said my name, Daddy stepped around me, took the boy's hand and spoke his name, then introduced Mama.

Lanier Thompkins had a swarthy complexion. His deep-set eyes appeared bruised and mapped with tiny, red veins. His was a tortured, tormented look I would see again and again as I met other young people who had undergone treatment after treatment, surgery after surgery. Each tried to hide the look through exuberant personality or self-conscious silence, never accomplishing the goal completely, but trying desperately.

Lanier Thompkins announced to Mama and Daddy that I was in good hands. "George Washington here watches after us like an old mother hen," he said, motioning toward the orderly.

When a plump nurse with rosy cheeks rushed up, bouncing to a stop in front of us, Lanier Thompkins arched his brows high and said, "And the nurses here are stormtroopers."

"Lanier, you devil, you," the nurse said in a syrupy, magnolia-laced drawl. "You get sour because we're so sweet to you." Nurse Lucy Greene smiled. "We spoil these children just too much sometimes. Now, Lanier, let me show these folks our facility."

Thompkins jerked his chair sideways, threw up his right hand in a salute, and snapped, "Yah volt, sergeant."

When he rolled through an opening between two curtained walls, his hairy arms bulged with muscles.

Watching him disappear, Nurse Lucy Greene said, "Lanier's truly a sweet boy." She lowered her voice and spoke confidentially, "But he is having a terrible time with a degenerative hip. He's had three surgical procedures and faces that many more. It seems never-ending sometimes."

Mama winced.

"How old is he?" I asked in a shaky voice.

"Sixteen," she said.

I gazed into the space where he had disappeared. I would have sworn he was at least eighteen. His voice was as hard as his mannerisms.

Lucy Greene guided us through the high-ceilinged room cut into sections by movable iron rods shaped into rectangles with white curtains stretched to form portable walls. We moved through the maze, where she introduced us to other nurses and children in beds. It was a white-on-white world. The walls were white. The curtained dividers were white. The people wore white. Even the light that shone through the windows was white.

While we moved quietly from place to place, I noticed—first out of the corner of my eye—a girl lying on a horizontal platform with a white metal cylinder covering her body from the tops of her shoulders to her bony calves. As we followed Lucy Greene into another curtained-off section, I turned to look back at the girl in the iron lung. She looked up into a mirror tilted at an angle above her head. I wanted to ask the nurse about her, but I held my words locked inside.

We moved through the cubicles, closer and closer to the girl with the apparatus that breathed in and out, in and out, rhythmically squeezing. Her skin was as soft and white as Lanier's was dark and hairy.

When nurse Lucy Greene finally approached the girl in the machine, she reached out and gently touched the auburn hair matted atop the girl's head resting on a white pillow. "This is Sara Jane," Lucy Greene said. I glanced into the reflection in the mirror. The image of a girl's face gazed directly at me. Her eyes were dark and brooding. Her mouth, painted a deep red, turned into an eager smile.

I mouthed, "Hello," and I saw her lips move, but I didn't understand her word.

I swallowed hard and moved away, following Mama and Daddy and the nurse to another part of the children's clinic. I glanced back once and caught a glimpse of her eyes in the mirror following me, and I felt instant guilt about something, but I couldn't pinpoint why.

As we moved through the ward room I realized the smell here was a different odor from the waiting room. A pine-scented fragrance of disinfectant permeated the atmosphere tinged with alcohol, the smell of medicines, and the odoriferous whiff of body waste.

The nurse led us down a hallway and through an open door into a twelve-by-twelve room dominated by a metal-frame bed. Like the large ward room, this world was also white.

Opening her arms, Lucy Greene announced, "This will be your home for the next few months," a statement that entered my body like a long syringe piercing my ears, puncturing my consciousness.

I looked from corner to corner, across the white spread on the white bed to the mound of white pillows, while Mama scurried over and opened the door to a closet against the far wall and Daddy handed her a sack with some of my things. Daddy said he'd get my suitcase which, for some reason, we'd left in the car. I could not think about the whys of anything at that moment. My mind felt like it had been packed with white gauze, without substance, empty.

It hit me: I will be here not tonight, not tomorrow, not the next day, not one week, but months. When you're fourteen, soon to be fifteen, a month is an eternity. I had never allowed myself to think about the time the doctor had said "a year out of your life." I hadn't given it a moment's thought, not allowing my mind to settle on it, not daring to count the days, the weeks. But now, suddenly, it was on me; the time weighed heavily, crushing down on my brain, the woman's words echoing with meaning, and it suddenly seemed forever.

I sighed, letting my breath seep from my lungs.

"Son?"

When I looked into her face, flushed with concern, I felt helpless.

"Are you all right?" she asked.

I nodded. "I'm fine," I lied.

I sat on the bed and looked toward the wall and the ceiling directly in front of the bed. A television set was anchored to the wall. It leaned toward the bed and was the only thing breaking the white monotony, other than some mechanical apparatus against the headboard and a floorlamp between the bed and a plastic-covered chair. Two other straight-back chairs sat in the far corner near a white-painted steam heater.

"Imaginative decoration," Daddy said.

Lucy Greene looked at him quizzically.

"I've seen insane asylums with more color," Daddy continued.

"Harold!" Mama said.

"Well, you'd think they'd hang a picture or something, just to give the place a little pizzazz."

"Well, I have nothing to do with the color scheme," Lucy Greene said.

Daddy said, "I'm glad of that."

"Harold!" Mama said again, her voice a little sharper.

Lucy Greene disappeared out the door. I wondered if Daddy had run her away for good. But she reappeared moments later with a stethoscope around her neck and a blood pressure gauge in her hands. She slid a cold glass thermometer between my lips and began wrapping the canvas sleeve around my left bicep. After she read my temperature she pressed her thumb to my wrist and began gazing at her watch, counting silently, her lips barely moving. Then she pumped a rubber bulb a half-dozen times, checking a gauge as the canvas sleeve tightened against the muscle. When she finished the process that would be repeated time and again every day, Daddy asked, "He gonna live?" with a chuckle edging his voice.

She threw Daddy a look of disgust, turned on her heel, told me to get into my pajamas, and left with her equipment.

As soon as she was gone, Daddy said, "Not much of a sense of humor."

"You didn't have to be so smart with her, Harold," Mama said.

A moment later, George Washington rapped lightly at my door. A smile played on his big face. "Nurse Greene told me to bring you this," he said, holding up a hospital gown. It too was white. "But you don't have to wear it until they start with the cast. And that won't be for a day or two. You can wear your p.j.'s 'til then."

George Washington, almost a head taller than Daddy and not half as big around, looked around wide-eyed.

Mama was fussing about, unpacking my suitcase, and Daddy was reaching up to turn on the television.

"Anything I can do for you?" the orderly asked.

"I can't think of anything," I said.

"Anytime you want me, you push that buzzer right over your head," he said. "Whatever you want, ol' George'll do it."

By the time I buttoned my pajama top, Mama and Daddy were standing on each side of the bed with nothing to do but stare down at me.

Mama patted my side softly. Daddy touched my knee.

I stared straight ahead into the face of a news commentator who talked in a modulated drone.

"We better go," Mama said in a strained, tight voice, like she wanted to say more but the words would not come.

"We'll be back tomorrow," Daddy said.

I nodded. I didn't know what to say, what to ask, what to do. I loved them so much, I couldn't say the words. I wanted them to go, but I didn't want to be alone. I felt scared, but I didn't know how to express fright. If I said anything, the words might crack and turn to tears, then I'd be in a hell of a mess. If I did that, Mama would break inside too. So I kept my words to myself, feeling tears already welling behind my eyes.

I reached out and touched both of their hands.

Mama's fingers played nervously with my fingers. Daddy laid his hand on top of mine.

I glanced up into their faces. My vision didn't linger. Both gazed down at me. I switched my eyes to the television and held there, looking at a scene of boys and girls filing through a museum somewhere looking at an art exhibit. I didn't hear what the announcer said.

After what seemed like a long time Mama and Daddy said goodbye and moved through the doorway into the hall, where I heard them talking to the nurse, asking when they could come back tomorrow. Then I heard their footfalls down the hallway, finally vanishing in the distance.

I was alone.

The sound of the television filled the chasm without meaning.

A sudden sadness overwhelmed me. I turned and pushed my face into the pillow and wept. I don't know how long I cried. My shoulders shook with grief over myself.

After I crossed a bridge between sorrow and ravished loneliness, I turned onto my back and wiped my face on the crisp fresh sheet, slid out of bed, wrapped a robe around my shoulders, and ventured into the hall in search of Lanier Thompkins.

F i v e

As I stepped into the children's ward I heard a murmuring rapture of voices and the wheezing-and-sucking rhythm of the iron lung. I stepped forward gingerly, wondering which of the cubicles belonged to Lanier. Halfway down the center aisle, a curtain to my left parted and his wheelchair rolled out and screeched to a halt.

His huge head cocked to the side, his bushy brows arched high over his mottled forehead, and his eyes glittered like they were afire with a green light. "What do you say, Thomas?" he said in his broadcaster's voice.

Without my replying, he said, "I can tell."

"You can tell what?"

"You stand crooked-shouldered," he said.

I tried to straighten myself, just as I had when Mr. Brainlevel the scoutmaster first spotted my physical predicament.

"You can't help it," he said. "Might as well wait until the surgery-mad sawbucks get finished with you. They'll have you standing straight as a board in a month or two. See how they've fixed me up," he said sardonically, throwing back his robe and lowering his pajama bottoms to reveal a crisscross of scar tissue that rose like a massive tattoo across his left hip.

The sight of blood-red stitching sent a wave of nausea through me as I stared dumb-eyed at him.

"It is a damn sight, isn't it?" he said.

When I said nothing, he said, "Well, you don't have to examine every inch of my ass," and pulled his pajamas up and slapped shut his robe.

He twisted his chair to the side and barked, "Follow!"

He led me to another, larger opening where tables and chairs sat in precise rows. "Let's have our dinner together," he said. He motioned for me to sit, and I pulled out a chair while he fixed himself at the head of the table. "I'll summon George Washington," he said, taking a buzzer from his breast pocket. "Handy little doohickey, when you have an emergency, which I have been known to have on occasion."

Appearing, George Washington stood like a tall, black genie. His eyes big and round, he listened as Lanier told him our plans.

"Sounds good to me," George said, smiling.

After he left, Lanier said, "George Washington is a damn good man. You can depend on him. Sometimes we depend on him too much. Sometimes he just does things for us, before we even ask, like he's reading our minds."

"You know your way around this place," I said, looking around the large room, seeing no one else but hearing them in the various cubicles hidden by the thin, curtained walls.

Outside the four high windows above the girl's mechanical lungs, the world turned dark. When I was a little boy, when I lived on the farm with my mother's parents, Granddaddy and Nanny, while Daddy was away in the Army during World War II, I liked to watch the sun go down over the trees west of our house. The way it settled on the horizon, turning yellow, then orange, and finally red, melting into the earth, always left me with a melancholy feeling, thinking sometimes that my father, no matter where he was at that instant, was watching the same thing that I was seeing, and that he was thinking about me and

Mama. Later, my little brother, Donnie Lee, came into the picture, and he was added to my thinking. Somehow, I always wondered about him and hoped that he was safe, wherever he was, especially when he was not with me, like now. But tonight I had paid no attention at all to the setting sun. I would realize in the days ahead that inside a hospital is not a place from which to view a sunset.

I looked beyond Lanier through an opening toward the girl who was being tended by several Negro women in uniforms. They wore gray-shaded dresses and matching aprons.

As they lifted the girl's thin legs that appeared no bigger than a solitary bone, a quick odor of defecation followed by a strong toxic sting of alcohol and ointment floated over us.

Lanier made a face and shook his head. "You never grow accustomed to the late afternoon nursing activities," he said. "It follows, just as surely as the sun goes down, that poor Sara Jane's daily mess will be cleaned by her private helpers. It's a pre-dinner whiff. Appetizing? I think not. Let us pray that George Washington will not appear with tonight's gourmet delights until the cloud has passed."

As soon as he said the words the orderly came through the door. He carried two trays with dishes covered with aluminum tops.

"Shall we allow our dinners to seep in their own fragrance for a few minutes longer?" Lanier said.

George Washington caught the drift, glanced toward the girl in the machine, and withdrew his hands from our trays. "As you wish," he said, moving away toward the girl and her helpers, pulling the curtain shut behind him.

"Thank God for small favors," Lanier said.

As we ate salisbury steak with gravy, mashed potatoes, green beans, a roll, and cherry Jello for dessert, all managing somehow to taste gooey, like plastic food from a metal container, Lanier told me about Sara Jane Matthews. "Poor little dear has lived in that damn iron lung most of her short life."

A year older than I, although she looked like a baby, her limbs and body never developed like most people's. Sara Jane Matthews was a child of wealth. Her father was a giant among Birmingham industrialists. He was the scion of a family that inherited much of the steel industry that developed in the iron-rich hills of the Magic City in the early years of the twentieth century. Sara Jane's mother was an attractive socialite who met her husband at an Ivy League college where both were students. The family lived in a brick mansion on wooded acres in the posh suburb of Mountain Brook. Sara Jane's older sisters were cheerleaders, darlings of their sororities; her older brother was the handsome star of his football squad. Sara Jane had been the fourth and last child, and after she was stricken with infantile paralysis and polio rendered her lungs useless, her parents deposited her in this place for crippled children. Sometimes the family visited on Sunday afternoons, after church and lunch at Joy Young's, a downtown Chinese restaurant that was an institution where well-to-do families dined when they weren't taking brunch at the country club. Sara Jane had been part of the family's weekend ritual when they weren't at their lake place or vacationing abroad or just had too much to do elsewhere. Their Sunday afternoon visits became fewer and fewer, until now the mother came about once a month and the father accompanied her quarterly. A team of Negro women were paid to keep an around-the-clock vigil on the girl who lived in the machine. "Every time Everett Matthews writes their checks, he feels the guilt escape through the throbbing pores of his arthritic right hand," Lanier said, his words thick with sarcasm. "Sara Jane is a prime example of the maxim: out of sight, out of mind."

The silent women in their uniforms combed Sara Jane's dark red hair a hundred strokes in the morning and again at night. They changed her diapers at least three times daily, and occasionally, usually on Sundays, they applied makeup to her sallow cheeks. She did not have the strength to hold a book above her face, but Lanier read to her from contraband literature. "Our current paperback masterpiece is *From Here to Eternity* by James Jones," he said. "Have you read it?"

I shrugged, shaking my head.

"When we finish, I'll bring it to you. Maybe you'd like to sit with us this evening?"

I glanced toward the curtained wall that George Washington had closed. I shrugged again.

"If you'd like . . ." He checked the gold watch on his left wrist. ". . . we'll start in about forty minutes. At seven."

"I'll try," I said. "I better go back to my room now."

On my way I passed another boy in a wheelchair. He smiled and said, "Hello," and I responded. His right leg had been amputated at the knee. A fat girl in a wheelchair stared at me. She had three chins and bulbous cheeks. Her eyes blinked as I gazed down at her hairless head.

I walked quickly, trying to escape before meeting someone else. But when I passed the last cubicle I glanced in to see George Washington lifting green beans on a fork, putting it gingerly into the mouth of a boy who had no arms.

By the time I reached my room I thought I was going to throw up. I went directly into the bathroom. I leaned over the commode. My stomach felt ticklish, but nothing came. I sat on the stool and cupped my palms over my middle and closed my eyes.

This is only the beginning, I told myself.

I lay down and stared up into the ceiling covered with squares of soundproof tile indented with small holes.

I closed my eyes.

Moments later, I argued with myself, thinking: I will not feel sorry for myself.

I flashed my eyes open, pushed up from the bed, and walked back into the big room. Beyond Sarah Jane's curtain Lanier Thompkins was reading in a low voice. I parted the curtain, peeped inside.

He stopped, looked up, and motioned for me to enter.

As I got settled in a seat behind her head, I saw her big brown eyes staring at me anxiously in the reflection in the mirror. She mouthed, "Hello," and I smiled and said, "Hey."

"This is the new boy I was telling you about, Sara Jane," Lanier said.

She worked her lips into a smile.

Lanier continued reading the passage of *From Here to Eternity*, describing the intense relationship between the wounded private, Robert E. Lee Prewitt, and the prostitute he loved, Alma. Just hearing the word "prostitute" sent a chill of excitement through my mind.

After the death of his friend Maggio, Prewitt had attacked Maggio's killer, the stockade sergeant Fatso, in an alleyway in Honolulu. While struggling with Fatso, Prewitt was bludgeoned with a knife. Now, recuperating at Alma's apartment, "it hit him hard. So hard that tears came into his eyes and he remembered, again, suddenly, how much he loved her, and went over and sat down and kissed her and put his hand on her breast solid-soft under the silk pajamas.

"She woke immediately, and was so immediately angrily horrified to find him out of the bed." As he spoke the words my eyes traveled from the page held in Lanier's open palms to Sara Jane's pasty face that colored pink. Then she giggled with timid delight, like a tiny bird's twitter.

I sat and listened, not quite understanding everything I heard, having come into the tale in the middle of some risque action. I had never cared for love stories. To me, they were always mushy and ridiculous. In fact, I'd never read much; most of the books and stories were childish things, fantasy and beyond. But this was real stuff between adults caught in the middle of a terrible situation that promised to get worse. A real fright permeated the pages. When Lanier finished the chapter, he closed the ragged paperback book, carefully marking the place and slipping it into a hiding spot under the bank of windows.

Lanier then introduced me and Sara Jane properly. "Soon he too will be a captive of the medical magistrates," Lanier told her, saying I would be covered with a body cast from the top of my head down to my knees. "Then Thomas will be more like you and me. He will know the real truth of this place."

Her eyes, big as silver dollars, gazed into my face. When I looked into her eyes I felt as though they were deep pools of brown water, depthless. No matter how long I stared into them, I would never see the bottom.

Her smile was not captivating. It was almost grotesque. Her teeth were too big for her mouth. Her lips were thin lines. Her pale skin was pulled tight over dainty bones, like a baby bird's.

As Lanier twisted his chair in a half-circle, turning with one move, knowing his limitations and the extravagance of his movements, he reached out and stroked her cheek with the back of his fingers. "See you later, kid," he said, and her gaze in the tilted mirror followed us from the cubicle as we passed two of the Negro women in their gray uniforms.

He came with me to my room, where I sat on the bed. "Will she ever . . ." I started.

Frowning, he shook his head. "She'll never escape that damned contraption," he said. "Never!" he said loudly. "It's a goddamn shame too. You ought to see those sisters of hers. Spoiled brats. Tits and ass. No brains. And their boy friends, whom they drag up here now and then, are dumber than the bitches. When I think about it, seeing her lying there helpless, wanting so much to learn and be a part of the world, wanting to escape her life sentence of torture, never being able to do anything for herself, not even breathing for herself, for God's sake."

The words spewed. He was in the middle of his harangue when George Washington poked his head through the door. "Don't get yourself in such an uproar about little missy," Washington said. "She'll be awright, long as her mama and daddy pay the bills."

"Bullshit," Lanier said.

"And quit yo' cussing so much."

Lanier's face masked with pain. "When I curse, I feel liberated, George."

Washington's face spread with a toothy grin, his eyes lighting. "It takes more'n that for me to feel my freedom. Reckon I been too long in the shackles to turn the key with just plain cussin'."

Lanier's cheeks went lax, his large face picturing gloom, his dark eyes shadowing. "I just wish there was something I could do for her," he said.

"I know," George Washington said. "We all do what we can. You read to her and tell her stories. I try to bring joy in the little ways I know."

"But her goddamn mama and . . ."

"Now, Lanier," the orderly said, his eyes softening, staring into the young white boy's face. "They do what they can."

"They're so rich they could buy a hospital especially for her. "

"And what good would that do?"

"She'd have everything at her disposal."

"She wouldn't have you, or me, or her other friends in yonder."

Lanier twisted his wheelchair ninety degrees with a quick jerk of his wrist, the muscles in his arms bulging, his mouth clamping shut, his tight jaw ticking like the second-hand of a clock.

"Lanier," George Washington said.

"I'm going back to her," Lanier said, rolling toward the door. "I want to tell her something before sleepy time."

Before exiting, he braked suddenly. He clamped his hands onto the chair's arms, raising himself up, pulling up with the strength of his Popeye's arms. He pivoted his body around to face me. "Thomas?" he said.

"Yeah?" I said.

"I'm going to tell her you'll help."

"Help?" I didn't understand.

He glanced toward the orderly, then back at me. "I'll tell you later."

"Don't mind me," George Washington said. He moved to leave.

Lanier shook his head emphatically. "No, you stay with Thomas, George. I'm going to see Sara Jane and tell her Thomas will come to her tomorrow."

"I will?" I said.

"Won't you?"

I nodded, not knowing what he expected.

Then Lanier lowered himself back into the chair and continued on his way.

As soon as his chair turned into the children's clinic, George Washington said, "Don't mind Lanier's cussin'. He's had a hard time of it these last few months."

"The surgery on his hip?"

"That's part of it," the orderly said. "The surgery has pretty much been unsuccessful. The doctors keep working on him, cuttin' and trimmin'. But that's not what's really and truly bugging him."

I stared into George Washington's pensive face. There was something regal about the way he stood straight and tall, his back flat against the white wall, his ebony skin taut against high-cut cheekbones that could have belonged to an old Indian chieftain, his wide African nose, his thick lips, his square-chiseled chin. He looked at me the way Brother Will had looked at me when he was explaining some deep and abiding truth of The Holy Bible, looking beyond the tender, ignorant truth of my exterior and seeing what lay inside.

"His mama and daddy ain't been to see him in the last two months. They been off on some kind of business trip to the Orient, Japan or someplace. They call from time to time to check on him, but it ain't like being here. He puts on a good front, pretending tough, pretending he's mad at Sara Jane's parents, pretending his own family life don't irritate and dig into him."

I listened to the man's words and pictured Lanier Thompkins different from the way I'd seen him just moments earlier. I listened to what he said and thought what it would be like if Mama and Daddy didn't make the trip from Tuscaloosa to Birmingham tomorrow just to say hello and be with me for a few minutes.

I thought about Lanier's brash manner, his over-loud voice, his tenderness with Sara Jane, his abrupt movements, the way he sat high in the wheelchair.

"You mind if I stand here for a while and watch *The Lone Ranger* with you?" George Washington said.

"No, of course not," I said. "Have a seat."

"I'll just stand here behind the door," he said. From where he stood, behind the open door, he was hidden from the hallway. I noticed his eyes flicker now and then from the action on the television screen to the hall, where he could spot someone coming.

"Temperature. Blood pressure. Pulse."

A new nurse opened the door to my room. She was younger than Lucy Greene, who was following her and telling her the routine. Strawberry blonde with a pert nose and a generous mouth painted pink around shining white teeth, she looked more like a movie star than a nurse. But she wore the white uniform and carried the equipment.

I had awakened a half-hour earlier, smelling scrambled eggs, fried bacon, and burning toast. I lay still and looked up into the soundproof ceiling, thinking that I should be home, hearing Mama holler, "Donnie Lee! Thomas! Get up and get ready! We've got to leave in a few minutes. If you don't get up now, you won't have time for breakfast." Instead, I heard a distant voice over a speaker in the hallway calling for Dr. Johnson in the ER. I heard bedpans and glass jars clinking somewhere in the ward-room. I heard a child crying.

"Thomas, this is Nurse Elizabeth. She's new to the hospital. Just down from Nashville, where she finished training. She'll be joining us on the sixth floor, working seven to three this week, when she'll be taking care of you and others."

Nurse Elizabeth smiled prettily. I smiled back.

I opened my mouth to accept the thermometer.

Her body emitted a warmth as she brushed against me. A slight hint of a sweet perfume touched my nostrils as I caught a glimpse of a lacy bra when the lapels of her uniform parted.

I took a deep breath. My teeth clinked against the glass stick.

She lifted it from my mouth, read it, then shook it before returning it to the holder, which she put into her breast pocket like a fountain pen.

She reached for my wrist, pulled it toward her, and clamped it in her grip. She frowned as she squeezed, looking at her wrist-watch.

"You should check his pulse while the thermometer is in his mouth," Nurse Lucy instructed.

Elizabeth glanced toward her, then back at her watch. She shifted her hold on my wrist.

I knew she had lost count of my pulse. I tried to relax to make it easier for her. I felt her hands grow clammy.

"Hold him firmly, but gently," Lucy said.

Elizabeth almost dropped my hand.

I stiffened against her.

Her body twittered against me. I could feel her nervousness tighten while she fixed her eyes on the second hand and counted silently. At least she didn't move her lips the way Lucy had yesterday. I almost smiled.

Momentarily, she dropped my hand, wrote a notation on the chart, and moved to wrap the sleeve around my upper arm.

She squeezed it so tight I thought she would cut off circulation. I watched as she squeezed the bulb, my arm being strangled by the pressure.

Lucy stepped to the bed, took hold of my arm, tried to work her finger between the sleeve and my skin, then turned toward Elizabeth and snapped, "Not so tight! Wrap it firmly! Not tight! You are looking for his pressure."

Elizabeth, with hands working up my arm, awkwardly unwrapped the sleeve and began again.

This time she left it so loose it could not squeeze tight enough to measure the pressure adequately.

This time, instead of rushing to me, Lucy inched away and regarded the younger nurse's work with a cold, hard eye.

While Elizabeth wrapped my arm the third time I could feel her fingers slip and slide. I tried to help by keeping my arm absolutely still, but she apparently thought I was pulling against her. She grabbed my biceps in her fingers and clamped the thumb, then swung the sleeve between my arm and body, pulling it together and tucking it. When she squeezed the bulb I lifted my arm toward her.

Her mouth clamped shut, hiding her pretty teeth. Her blue eyes squinted as she concentrated on the gauge that registered my blood pressure.

Mission accomplished, Elizabeth sighed audibly and released my arm. Before writing in my chart, she glanced into my face. Pure exasperation and instant relief filled her eyes. I smiled, but she didn't return the gesture.

Lanier Thompkins came to fetch me for breakfast. "I've got to talk with you," he said as we entered the large room.

As we moved between the curtained rooms we heard the sounds of movement, of moans and groans, of pained grunts, of people being moved, of beds being stripped, of knives and forks working, of the world starting a new day.

We sat at the table where we had had dinner. A black woman in a white uniform brought our breakfast trays. While we ate, Lanier said, "I told Sara Jane you would visit her this evening."

"To do what?" I asked.

"It would be nice if y'all got to know each other."

I shrugged. "I'd like to know her," I said.

"She is really a sweet person," he said.

"She looks sweet to me."

"She needs a boy friend."

"Now, Lanier, wait a minute. I just got here. How do you know I don't already have a girl friend."

"You don't look like someone who has a girl friend."

I stared into his splotched face, the clown-like features darkening. This boy who had become my friend before I was settled into my room, before I knew my way around this place, before I got to know anyone else on the sixth floor, was now directing my life.

"Lanier, I don't want to hurt her," I said, trying to think of something to say, some way to react without hurting him as well.

"How would being friendly hurt her?" he asked. He was the innocent buddy suggesting a friendship that would help me and help this poor girl. He wanted to do what he thought best for both of us. He pushed. "What the hell? Day after tomorrow you'll be bound up in a body cast, confined to your bed. She will continue to live in that damned machine that breaths for her. You will be jailed in your room. She will be lying there beneath the big windows. Each of you will be able to think about the other. I thought that perhaps . . ." He let his voice trail off, gazing at me with those big dark green eyes, letting me imagine whatever series of words might follow.

"Tell her I will come to her just before the sun sets," I said.

"You don't have to do it," he said, his voice twisting the words.

"I'll be there, just before the sun sets."

"They clean her just after the sun goes down."

"Tell them to do it early today." I stood and walked down the corridor between the curtained rooms. I went to my room where two men dressed in white waited with a gurney to take me to x-ray.

The day was filled with tests. I was hauled from floor to floor. The men twisted me and turned me, x-raying my chest, my front side, my back, my right side and my left. They x-rayed me sitting and standing, lying down, propped against a wall, and standing between two machines. Nurses took blood from my fingers and my arms. A specialist examined my throat. Another rammed a tube up my rectum. Nobody explained why.

After Mama and Daddy brought me another Ollie's barbecue and a Coca-Cola for lunch, a man came to the room and measured my height, the circumference of my head, my chest, my waist, each of my arms, and my thighs. The same two men who had taken me to x-ray rolled me to a testing area where wires were attached to my chest, stomach, back, and three places on my neck. I was told to walk on a moving platform that rose at a steeper and steeper slant, until I was trudging uphill. Then it lowered, and the speed was increased until I had to trot to keep from being thrown backward.

Back at my room, I checked the time.

Mama and Daddy sat in chairs on opposite sides of my bed.

"Y'all going back tonight?" I asked.

"We have to," Mama said. I knew she was tired. Daddy too. Their eyes looked weary when they first entered my room at eleven-thirty this morning. They'd probably stayed up too late last night. Probably arguing. Probably about me.

She said they would be leaving, but they didn't make a move to go.

I slid my legs off the edge of the bed, put my feet into my slip-pers, and began slipping into my robe. "I've got something I've got to do," I said.

"They've given you all the tests for today, haven't they?" As usual, there was an edge to Mama's voice.

"They've tested me more ways than you want to know, Mama," I said.

"Well . . ."

"Well, I've got to go spend some time with someone in the big room."

"Do I detect a slight hint of female in the air?" Daddy asked. I shot him a look.

"My boy's got a girl friend already."

"I have a friend," I said.

"Well, why didn't you say?" Mama said.

"I've just been here . . ."

"My boy's a fast worker. In the hospital twenty-four hours, he's already got something on the line."

"Harold!"

What can I say? I asked myself. Where can I go? Where can I hide? It's either them or Lanier. My problems are multiplying.

I walked out, leaving them in my room to steep in their dis-cussion of whatever they thought I might be up to. By the time I peeped through the parted curtain at Sara Jane's cubicle, I had made up my mind to tell her straight-out that I wasn't looking for a girl friend. I had never had a girl friend, although I'd had a half-dozen dates with Mary Russell Simmons, whom I had known for four years and who lived down the street and didn't expect me to be more than what I was. Mary Russell and I had gone to several Friday night movies together, attended the annu-al dance at junior high when I wore a dinner jacket, cummerbund, and bowtie and Mary Russell wore a frilly, long pink gown. I spilled catsup on my new white shirt and Mary Russell almost tripped on the hem of her dress during the leadout. We had our picture made under the arbor of artificial flowers and the banner reading: HAPPY CLASS 1954.

Making sure the private nurses were no longer hovering over Sara Jane, I pulled the curtain back and stepped into the cubicle. I moved slowly toward the machine that pumped up, pushed down, making its rhythmical sucking and wheezing sounds.

She twisted her head, her big eyes trying to find me. When our eyes met, I said, "Hey," and she mouthed, "Hi."

The nurses applying lipstick had strayed from the lines of her mouth. The bright red was too heavy in the corners, giving her a twisted, affected look. The shadow around her eyes did not accentuate the brown but made them appear darker, funny-sinister. The smells of alcohol and Vaseline filled the air, mixed with a light fragrance of perfume and the metallic smell of grease on the pistons of the machine.

As I neared, she whispered, "I know I look a fright."

"No, no," I said softly. "You look . . . fine."

Her lips rubbed together and she closed her eyes. She was trying to mask the pain.

"I think you look fine," I said, trying to reassure her.

She opened her eyes and looked up at my reflection in her mirror. She blinked.

"Did Lanier read to you today?"

She nodded almost imperceptibly.

"You like it?"

"It's very sad."

"I never have read much."

"It's sad, and very real. I think these cross-ups actually happen to people in real life."

"What kind of 'cross-ups'?"

"How a person can be married to one person and fall out of love and find another person they really do love but they are afraid to make a real commitment. Everybody thinks everybody else knows what they're thinking, what they're feeling, but they don't."

I didn't say anything, trying to wade through what she had said.

"You know, how two adults are married for a long time but instead of becoming closer and feeling more love, it seems they are growing farther and farther apart?"

I nodded the same way she had.

She kept her eyes glued to my reflection.

"Then, say, the wife finds someone who is kind and gentle to her? And they have an affair? But pretty soon the affair becomes meaningless because there is no real commitment?"

"You mean, to marriage? To divorce? And then marriage?"

Again, she did her little nod. "Yeah, or just being together like husband and wife."

I was not sure I understood precisely what she meant. It was something to think about.

As I looked into her delicate little oval face, staring into the dark-shadowed eyes, I saw something much deeper than just sad-funny. She appeared to be a child but thought with a wiser knowledge. Her brain questioned the possibilities of a world I had never even imagined.

"It's a very complicated story about a whole bunch of individuals caught up in an intriguing web of human weaknesses," she said.

Gazing at her in a wonder, she suddenly smiled brightly. "Those aren't my words," she confessed.

"Oh?"

"It's what Lanier told me. I think he read it off the book's cover. Or maybe an advertisement."

"Oh."

"He also said something about Private Prewitt, Sergeant Warden, Karen Holmes, Alma, Maggio, Fatso, and all the others illustrating the human condition at its most vulnerable—in the days just before the beginning of a great war."

"What does that mean?" I asked.

She continued to smile. "They're in a world of shit," she said. I chuckled.

"As Maggio might say, 'We're all fucked-up.' "

I didn't know how to reply. I'd never heard a girl say such words.

Later, in my room, I told Lanier Thompkins what I'd felt.

He twisted his chair abruptly. "Aw, shit, man! Did you tell her that?"

"No," I said. "I did not. I didn't want to embarrass her."

"Hell, you would have embarrassed yourself, you numbskull. Her words are perfectly natural. She says what she knows, what she believes. She's honest. You're the one who's fucked-up. Did you kiss her?"

"No," I said.

"Why not?"

"We just talked."

"You should have kissed her. Kiss her properly. Put your lips on her lips. Touch. Probe. Make her feel alive."

"Lanier, you're the one full of shit."

"I mean what I say," he said.

"Why don't you kiss her?"

"Me?"

"Yes, you. You're the one who reads *From Here to Eternity* to her. You're the one who knows her best. You're the one who is hurt by the way her family treats her."

"If I kissed her, Thomas, it'd be like her brother kissing her. Albeit, I would certainly be the most loving brother she has—by far. Still, a brother's kiss is weak, if you get my drift."

"But I've never kissed a girl, other than Mary Russell Simmons."

"Did you really kiss her?"

"We kissed."

"Not just a peck on the cheek?"

"It wasn't some kind of French kiss, if that's what you mean."

"I'm not going to give you some kind of post-graduate course in kissing, for God's sake."

"I know how to kiss," I said.

Lanier let it go for the time being. We talked about the Alabama Crimson Tide football team, which was terrible and getting worse with each game. We talked about the latest John Wayne movie, which I'd seen. Lanier said he'd read an article in *Confidential* magazine about movie actress Tallulah Bankhead, an Alabama girl, spending weekends on yachts naked as a jay-bird, entertaining British royalty. "At a party after the fling, when the lord with whom she'd been cavorting tried to ignore her, she said, 'What's the matter, dahling, don't you recognize me with my clothes on?' " We whooped.

Before Lanier left, after George Washington arrived and took his position behind my door, just in time to see the latest adventures of *Sky King*, Lanier said, "Tomorrow afternoon, just before twilight, you will go back to Sara Jane. You will touch her and you will kiss her. It will be your final chance."

"Don't tell her," I said.

"I won't," he said. "What do you think? I'm insensitive, or something?"

"Just don't get her hopes up."

"Who are you? John Wayne or somebody?"

"Lanier!"

"What?"

"I'll go to her."

In my darkest hour, I dreamed about what it might feel like to be encased in a body cast, but my imagination would not allow me to reach that far.

The next day was crammed full of tests, x-rays, blood samples, measuring my body, double-checking everything physical about me. Every section of the hospital had my statistics in triplicate.

All morning, while being wheeled down hallways amid other patients, I thought about my time with Sara Jane Matthews. I thought about how she looked when I first walked into her cubicle. I thought about the smells that tickled and teased and irritated my nostrils. I thought about her mouth and her eyes.

Mama and Daddy were waiting in my room when I arrived before lunch. The attendants allowed enough time for a meal before wheeling me through the next series of examinations.

I knew my parents had not had a restful night. I hoped that Donnie Lee had not had to suffer through too much. If he had, at least he was accustomed to it. He was ten. Mama's parents, Granddaddy and Nanny, had moved into the house on Magnolia Street in Tuscaloosa and were helping to take care of Donnie Lee and the house while Mama and Daddy were running back and forth to Birmingham to see about me.

All afternoon, while I made the rounds, I thought about my twilight visit with Sara Jane. I would not hesitate, like yesterday. I would step up to her. I would lower my head to her face. I would cradle her head in my firm and confident palms. I would press my lips to hers and hold them there, parting my lips and feeling her teeth. I would smell only her perfumed fragrance.

Her tongue would dart between my teeth. I would hear her sigh as her lips would eagerly tremble, desperately seeking my taste.

When I returned Mama and Daddy were sitting in my room. Mama was reading the latest *Reader's Digest* and Daddy's eyes were scanning a sports magazine. They sat on opposite sides of my bed. Mama asked about what all had happened that day. I began running through a litany of my daily activities, my words sharp and sarcastic in their repetition. When I finished, Mama's eyes shifted downward. "Well, I'm sorry," she muttered. As the hurt look crossed her face I wanted to reach out and grab my words and pull them back and stuff them deep down inside. But, of course, I couldn't. I had made my usual mistake of speaking too quickly. Daddy stood and moved to the window side of my bed, extending the magazine he had been perusing. "You read about the Tennessee football team?" he asked. I shook my head. "Looks like they're going to be pretty good this year," he said. Then he added, "And Texas A&M." I didn't really care about the Tennessee Volunteers or the Texas Aggies, but at least with him I held my words inside. I just shook my head slowly.

I got out of bed as quickly as I'd crawled into it. I excused myself.

Daddy said, "You going to see the same girl?"

I mumbled some sound and added, "I'll be back in a little while."

I moved down the hallway and into the cavernous, well-lighted wardroom. I saw Lanier at the far end and motioned toward him and he gave me the A-ok sign.

I found my way to Sara Jane's cubicle. I hesitated, listening. All I could hear was the rhythmical sound of her machine. I whiffed the flavor of medicine in the air, something that was foreign only twenty-four hours ago but was now as familiar as the fragrance of honeysuckle on Magnolia Street. I closed my eyes momentarily, examining once again my romantic plan as I approached her.

My eyes explored her face as I approached slowly. Her face had been scrubbed clean. Her complexion shimmered an alabaster shade of gray-white. Her eyes, minus the make-up, shone like giant opals set in sockets of tarnished silver. Her lips, without the garish red paint, pouted purplish under the glow of a pink sunset that cast its last light through the bank of windows.

Her eyes seemed to expand as I drew closer. Her lips moved.

I wanted to say something sweet and gentle, but words stuck in my throat.

I moved down toward her. I extended my hands, cupping my fingers. I reached for her head, wanting to cradle it.

I lowered my face toward hers, dropping slowly to her, gazing into the perfect heart-shape of her mouth.

Then I froze. I felt a fearful flutter in my stomach. I opened my own lips, shaping them.

I slid my face next to hers, turned, and pecked her cheek with a touch of my lips, barely raking against her silk-soft velvet cheek.

Then I closed my eyes, and when I looked again into her face, she was staring into my face, and her thin lips were puckering, making themselves ready.

A sick feeling overwhelmed me. I rose and backed away.

As I took each deliberate, hurtful step away from her, I was sure I heard her beg, quietly urging, "Please stay! Please!"

Hesitating a few feet away, a space that seemed suddenly a far, far distance, I clinched my teeth and sucked in a deep breath.

The harsh odor of the medicine swept through me and teased my insides. I knew I was going to be sick.

I turned and fled. When I passed Lanier in the corridor between the cubicles I looked blankly into his eyes and shook my head and said nothing as I strode in wide steps into the hall.

Before I reached the door to my room I remembered Mama and Daddy. I didn't want to face them. Not now. I wanted to run somewhere. I wanted to throw myself into a dark room and hide. I didn't want to see anyone. I wanted only to be alone.

I started to turn but found George Washington standing directly behind me. He reached out and took hold of my shoulder to keep me from running into him. His face showed surprise at my quickness. "Yo' mama and daddy are in your room talking with the doctor. They want you."

Without saying a word, I turned and walked to my room, entering as though everything in this world was in perfect alignment.

Dr. Albert Braswell, his bald head covered with a mint-green surgeon's cap, stood at the foot of my bed with a chart in his hands. When he saw me he flashed a smile. "Thomas, I was telling your parents what to expect tomorrow because tomorrow is your big day."

I nodded, still feeling the sickness that had hit me like a fist in the stomach.

I sat on the edge of the bed and listened as he explained the details of the procedure. When he finished he said, "Your parents will be waiting when they finish with the cast."

I nodded, having heard his words but feeling my brain turn to cement. Not thinking, I shivered and lay back. I started to push my feet under the covers and pull the sheet up to my chin.

Dr. Braswell said, "Don't you want to walk into the wardroom and have dinner with your friends? This will be your last up-right dinner in a long while."

Staring at him, I stopped all movement. I imagined that this was what it was like to have your last meal before the long walk to the electric chair. Everybody gazed at you and outlined morbid details, cold and clinical. To me, every detail spelled torture, pain, and agony, endless hours of monotony. They might as well take out a piece of wood and begin sharpening it, whittling it down all night until it was sharp enough to drive into my body between my heart and my spine while I lay awake all night listening to other workmen fit together pieces of wood being placed together in the perfect shape of a coffin into which my body would fit.

I rose, robed myself, and walked woodenly into the large cold room where the lights burned too bright, making all the white shine like it was brand new, hard on the eyes.

All of the nighttime sounds blended like the songs of crickets in the last glow of light in the forest near a pond. Beyond all the talk, the songs of moaning children being readied for bed, I heard the squish-squash rhythm of Sara Jane's iron lung pumping with a quiet, almost silent, desperation, the thread of noise that bound them together with a hope: as long as it sounded, there was life.

I saw Lanier Thompkins from a distance. He sat high in his wheelchair. I hoped he'd eaten and had to go back to his cubicle or had business in another part of the hospital. I did not want to look him in the face. I did not want him looking at me and seeing the coward he surely recognized.

I sat at the place at the table where I had eaten for the past two nights.

Hearing the roll of his wheelchair beside me, its sound as recognizable as heavy footfalls, I looked straight ahead, wishing that George Washington would appear out of nowhere with my tray.

Lanier jerked his chair to a halt, pulling it squarely to the end of the table. When I looked up and my eyes met his, he smiled a big toothy grin and said, "I guess you're destined to die a virgin."

I said nothing. I wanted to eat and get out. I did not need nor did I request his sarcasm. I felt that I had betrayed him as well as her. I felt heavy with remorse and apprehension. My entire being was burdened with my new life which I knew would change drastically tomorrow morning.

"You've got a lot on you," Lanier said. "The night before is always hard." He reached out and touched my arm. It was an amazingly gentle touch.

I looked into his pain-crusted face. His eyes, deep within the darkened and bruised sockets, glistened with dampness. I wanted to thank him, but I was afraid if I said a word I would burst into tears.

"I know how it is," he said.

It was enough.

When George Washington brought my tray I ate only half of the food.

When I rose to leave, Lanier said, "Don't worry. It'll be all right." But this time his words sounded empty, as though spoken into a drum.

E i g h t

I awakened in the middle of the night when a scream careened through the hallway. It sounded like a bobcat whose foot had been caught in an iron spring trap. In the woods in the North River country of Tuscaloosa County near the community of Samantha, when I was coon-hunting with Granddaddy and Uncle Baxter, we heard such a cry. The shriek shocked me then. And this time I bolted upright in the bed, immediately picturing Sara Jane Matthews.

I threw my legs off the side of the bed and began searching in the dark for my slippers when George Washington appeared at my door and said, "Everything's all right. Just lay back down now."

"But . . ."

"It's that little Calhoun boy who had cancer surgery yesterday morning. He woke up and rolled over on his incision."

The next time the scream was softer.

"They got him something to ease his pain," Washington said. "He's a poor little tyke, that one."

I remembered seeing him several times: a little wide-eyed youngster who had lost all of his hair. He was pale as a ghost and his eyes seemed bigger than Sara Jane's.

"They tried all the cobalt treatment they could give him, trying to kill them old cancer things eatin' up his body like they was termites in his heart. Only thing left to do, the doctors say, was to cut 'em out, and that don't always help things."

George Washington knew everything about everyone in the children's clinic. I was glad he was my friend.

"You all right now?" he asked, standing near the doorway.

I slid my feet under the covers. "Yeah," I said. "I'm all right."

He started to turn.

"George?" I said.

"Yes, sir," he answered.

"After tomorrow, will you come back and watch TV with me?"

The tall shadow of George Washington moved back into my room close to my bedside. He reached out and touched the hump of my left leg. "You can rest assured, Thomas, George Washington will be right here when you come back up from gettin' yo' cast on. I'll be here in time to see *Lone Ranger* and *Sky King*, and maybe we can even look at *I Love Lucy*, though I've noticed you're not too partial to that show."

"I'll watch it if you want to, George."

"Then me and you, we got us a date." He patted me again before he turned and eased away without a sound, closing the door.

Alone in the dark, I lay awake and stared up into the gray ceiling where now and then a shadow of something from outside and downstairs crept across the expanse.

I was thankful that the scream had not come from Sara Jane Matthews. I thought of her lying in that iron lung, looking at the same thing day in and day out, believing in some kind of fantasy enchantment dreamed up by her friend Lanier Thompkins, then that person who was supposed to perform the promised chores, a duty of love, failed miserably.

Guilt tore through me. I wanted to return to her, but I knew I couldn't. I wanted to rise up and go to her and lean over her and beg her forgiveness. What harm would it do if I cradled her head next to mine and ran my fingers through her silken hair and kissed her cheeks and the tarnished-silver sockets that held her deep brown eyes? Why couldn't I have lowered my face to hers, taken her tongue into my mouth, and kissed her with a passion that I felt now at three o'clock in the morning?

Finally, after thinking about her and Lanier and the little Calhoun boy and the other faces and bodies of children, I closed my eyes and slept restlessly.

I was awakened by Nurse Elizabeth flicking on the lights. "What?" I asked.

She went about her business in a quick manner: taking temperature, checking pulse, measuring blood pressure, then leaving silently. I took my last shower, soaping good and hard and long, rinsing longer. I ate a big breakfast with Lanier, who shook my hand and said he'd come to my room later today to check on me.

As I walked away from the tables, I glanced toward Sara Jane's cubicle. I saw the backsides of two of the women tending to her, both huddled around the machine that was pumping rhythmically. I did not see Sara Jane's face or even her profile. I walked down the long corridor to the hallway and to my room.

I took off my pajamas, slid into the hospital jacket, having a hard time fastening the ribbons behind my back, then I lay in my bed and waited: wonder filling my mind, my heartbeat racing, my imagination building, questions forming, thinking that the doctor was surely wrong about my having to stay in the body cast for months.

Finally, two strange orderlies came and lifted me onto a gurney. My gown fell apart. When I reached around to draw it together, they laughed and said, "Don't worry about that. After this trip you won't be able to wear the gown." I stared up into their playful eyes, feeling stupid.

They delivered me to a room on the third floor where a sour-faced man in a surgical uniform instructed them to put my naked body on a metal table. It was hard and cold. They turned me over onto my stomach. The man wearing the green tunic and loose-fitting green pants placed a piece of felt across my back. It reached from the top of my butt to the base of my neck. Then he began piecing slabs of wet gauze that smelled like damp clay, plastering it over the felt. Then he told the orderlies to turn me. The man wrapped the top of my body from my neck to below my navel with a dry matting. Then he placed swatch after swatch of plaster-soaked gauze in layers across my chest and stomach, then along my sides, and down over my left thigh to my knee. It grew heavier, thicker and thicker, until I could not move beneath the weight. The damp plaster cast covered my entire body. Holes were left for my arms. After he fixed the wrappings around my thigh, he returned with a sharp knife. My eyes rolling downward, I watched anxiously, holding my breath. I wanted to cross my legs to keep him away from my middle, but I couldn't. He reached down with the knife, like a butcher, and sliced away a sliver of cast next to my penis. Wearing rubber gloves, he pushed my scrotum to the side and carved away another sliver. For an instant, it felt as though he were cutting into my skin, then he backed off, examining his work from a distance.

Then he moved close again and asked me to lift my right knee. When I did he lowered his knife again and cut away a section next to my buttocks, and again he backed away and gazed squint-eyed at my midsection.

The cast began hardening even as the orderlies rolled me back to the room on the sixth floor. Mama met us at the door. She stepped to my side. Her eyes, eager to see me, betrayed her abrupt shock as she focused on my predicament. She sucked in a quick breath, not sighing but feeling quick pain at the sight. She blinked, turned, and backed away.

I knew I looked horrible. The metallic stench drifted up as the plaster hardened around me, my body sweating in the confines of the shell that enveloped me and held me captive.

The two orderlies positioned themselves at my head and my feet, reached out and took hold, then lifted me awkwardly up into the air and brought me down with a bounce onto the bed. My head spun lightly, like it was floating up and away, lighter than the cast.

A fever swept down through the cast. The heat wrapped around my body, and the flavor of my perspiration mixed with the sour smell of the drying plaster.

Quicker than my coating had been laid, my body emitted dampness, drenching me.

"My God, darling!" Mama muttered. She placed her hand on my forehead and withdrew it. "You're on fire!"

She snapped the button hanging from the headboard. She skittered away, disappearing into the bathroom, and reappeared with a rag. She leaned over my face and put the rag—cold and damp—to my forehead, then mopped it down over my nose and cheeks.

Nurse Elizabeth strolled in like she was going to a party.

"He's burning up," Mama said.

Nurse Elizabeth put the thermometer between my lips. She took my wrist in her small dainty white hand.

Withdrawing the glass stick from my mouth, she stared at it in amazement. "A hundred and one," she said.

As though he were psychic, George Washington appeared with a container of water and a bucket of chipped ice.

Mama took it, gave me a sip through a curved straw, and placed ice on my parched lips.

As quickly as I had grown hot and wet, a chill spread across my body. I shivered like I had been dropped into a hill of snow. The hardness of the plaster's interior that a moment earlier had burned my tender skin now froze it like a block of ice. I grabbed for blankets that George Washington held out to me. He pulled the covers up to my chin, where a plaster cup held it high and stiff, like an iron collar.

"Do something!" Mama snapped at the nurse, who was standing halfway between the bed and the door. The young woman's eyes widened, then she turned on the balls of her feet and scampered out the door.

"You need more covers?" George Washington asked.

I was shivering. I couldn't speak. When I opened my mouth my teeth clattered together.

He extracted another blanket from a closet and spread it over the bed.

No sooner than it fluttered down on top of me I caught a deep whiff of the stench from beneath the plaster. Heavy and rancid, it invaded my nostrils, turned my stomach, and this morning's scrambled eggs and bacon bolted up through my throat and played there nauseously until my stomach rumbled like a volcano.

As the vomit exploded from my lips, my mother screamed.

Through my tears I saw George Washington move Mama aside gently and lean over me with a towel, talking in a cool, clear, easy voice, "Now, Mrs. Morgan, don't get upset. Thomas'll be awright. I'll take care of everything."

He began cleaning me, gathering the new blanket he'd just dropped onto the bed into folds and wiping away the mess that had streamed down my cheeks and was now caking at the edge of the cast. Behind him, a team of nurses and more orderlies appeared in the doorway. Nurse Lucy took his place with Elizabeth on the opposite side.

As soon as they got me clean, I felt another eruption. I couldn't speak. I made a pained face, closed my eyes, and felt clothed in terror as I opened my lips and let it flow.

"Oh, my God!" Mama cried out again. "Isn't there something you can give him?"

Elizabeth squeezed my shoulder and slid a needle stinging into the flesh of my upper arm, squeezing a colorless liquid into my bloodstream. Lucy put a tablet onto my tongue and slid the crooked straw between my lips and whispered, "Suck."

When I opened my eyes the two nurses had moved back and allowed George and another orderly to work on my new mess, the smell enough to make anyone sick.

I lay miserably in my own vomit. Drenched in sweat, covered with chills, sated with medicinal fluids, my brain swam in a sea of discontent. I was unable to move.

I closed my eyes again and dreamed a dream of swirling colors, of a vast sea that glistened blue-green textures of semiprecious stones beyond a snow-white, sunbathed beach. And on that beach lay a beautiful, sublime, slender girl whose frail body, the color of milk, beckoned to me. She had long, silky, auburn hair and eyes that were brown as chocolate and wellmanicured nails painted the same bright red as her lips.

When I awakened I gazed up into the semidarkness at the high, tiled ceiling. I stared at the dots on the rectangular tiles. I counted the rows of tiles from the wall behind my bed to the wall on the far side. Then I counted the number of holes in each tile. Then I multiplied them. With the sum of the total floating in my head, my eyelids shut again and I dozed. When I awakened, I looked with bored interest into each of the four colorless corners of the room. In the far corner I spotted a spider creeping over the edge of the molding, high, high above me. Strong and mighty, the defiant insect was queen of her orderly world. She stepped spryly, inspecting the site, circling the corner, judging the territory over which she moved, like an engineer inspecting a place where he would build a dam or a building or a bridge. The spider was an artist exploring the possibilities on a canvas of particular dimensions, or a worker who knew the parameters of her abilities, the distances allowed by the reach of her natural tools. Amazed at her patience and perseverance, I watched each of her precise movements as she went about her business as though each step had been planned down to the tiniest detail.

Heavy with drugs, my eyes closed again. And again I dreamed of the pale pretty girl, now stretched upon a boulder high on a mountaintop, her long frail arms flailing against the turbulent air that swept around her like a small tornado. I tried to reach out and grab her as I floated past, but my speed and distance made it impossible to rescue her from whatever danger lurked there.

When I awakened abruptly Mama was picking particles of my sickness from the gauze-lined cup of plaster under my chin, and I tried desperately not to be sick again.

Daddy appeared with his long, clown-like face. He stretched his face longer than its usual horse shape, eyes bulging, but I did not find humor in his attempt. He produced a football signed by the entire University of Alabama Crimson Tide football team and held it out to me. I just stared at it and did not reach up to take it. I blinked tearfully and told him this year's team was the worst in Southeastern Conference history. His face fell, and I bit my lip, punishing myself. He placed the football on a shelf where some unread magazines lay, then he looked toward Mama, whose own sad face wrinkled helplessly. He moved to my bedside and slid his arm around Mama's waist and stared down at me with watery eyes. He held her close, saying nothing.

I wished they would leave. I felt sick and sad and hurtful and wanted to be alone in my misery. Why did I make them miserable too? I bit the inside of my lip again and tasted the coppery flavor of blood ooze down my throat. I was glad they had not brought my little brother, Donnie Lee, to see me in such a terrible way.

To escape their stares, I gazed up and found the spider at work, tying an end of her near-invisible web to a wall, pivoting on her dainty, bent legs, then dancing as though on tiptoes to another spot on the perpendicular wall.

My mind lost in the spider's work, I disregarded my parents' comments, their laments, their sorrows.

N i n e

Lanier Thompkins brought words of solace and concern from Sara Jane Matthews and a new paperback entitled *The Story of O* about a young female love slave kept in a castle where she was forced to do remarkably unspeakable acts that made my erotic brain swim out of control. Lanier said that Sara Jane was looking forward to my recovery when I could return to her and fulfill her dream and my promise. I nodded, thinking that the next time I would complete my mission. I would be a man in a world where men did not turn away from such a mission of honor, of love and fulfillment.

I awakened in the middle of the night, my body covered with sweat, picturing Sara Jane Matthews with breasts and legs, naked and lovely, stretched spread-eagle, begging to do anything I requested, all I had to do was ask, and I was hard and hot and throbbing. God! I cried out to myself.

One afternoon when I was reading the book, feeling the heat growing between my legs, Daddy appeared. He grinned and said, "What're you doing, sport?"

I dropped the book, shoving it beneath the covers.

"What're you reading?" he asked. "Something sexy?"

I clamped my lips shut. I prayed that my penis was not giving away my secret. I kept my arms stretched to the sides of the bulging cast, trying to hold the sheet high enough to cover my secret.

Daddy grinned. "I just thought I'd look in on you." From a brown paper sack he produced a magazine, like a magician pulling a rabbit from a hat.

He held it open, pushing it toward me, and I reached out with shaky hands.

Quivering before my eyes was a near-naked, gorgeous woman with shoulder-length, platinum-blonde hair, full red lips, large breasts with nipples pointing straight out.

"Some bazooms, ain't they?" Daddy asked, his eyes bulging, his wide mouth grinning.

I flushed red and quickly closed the magazine.

The nurse named Lucy came in and glared toward Daddy.

I shoved the magazine beneath the covers next to *The Story of O.*

Lucy pushed a thermometer into my mouth, going through the routine.

Behind her, Daddy, still grinning, winked at me.

I prayed that he would say nothing.

He didn't, until she turned away and started out. Then he said, "That one's got a cute bottom," making her turn and scowl with disdain. When she marched out she slammed the door.

Daddy giggled. "You got to show 'em who you are." He put his hand at the top of my head where the cast curved up over my matted hair. He patted, like he'd pet a dog. "And you're a man, Thomas Morgan." His eyes twinkled and he winked again.

"My present for you is a new magazine started a year or so ago. I found this year's February issue in Murray Applebee's barber shop down in Centreville. It's called *Playboy* and the centerfold is Jayne Mansfield. They say she's the new Marilyn Monroe. Something, ain't she?"

He strutted around the foot of the bed like a tall, big-breasted peacock, proud of himself. I wished harder that he would leave. I wanted to get back to the naked woman, to examine her with care, but I was not about to bring out the magazine while he was still lingering at my bedside.

When he asked if he could roll my bed up, I said, "No," sharply.

I knew I'd hurt his feelings again, and I started to bite my lip, but he shrugged and said, "I guess I better get back on the road and make us a living."

I started to say I appreciated his coming, but I didn't. He closed the door quietly, not bothering to come over and touch me or kiss me with his tobacco-speckled lips that smelled of smoke and menthol.

After I heard his footfalls receding down the hallway, I pulled out the magazine and stared into the round pale softness of the breasts of Jayne Mansfield sitting on the edge of a bathtub with her arms stretched above her head.

Later in the day, when I passed the magazine to Lanier, who stared unabashedly at the photos, holding them up to the light, he stated that my father was the greatest dad in the world. I remained silent, feeling guilty, while Lanier said, "What other father would bring his bedridden teenager such a treasure?"

George Washington made his appearance every day between five-thirty and six P.M., his face scrunched into a mask, winking as he slipped behind the door, where he stood to watch our favorite television shows and where he could keep a watch on the hall between my room and the children's ward.

"Lanier's depressed today," he confided. "Forty-fourth day he ain't heard from his folks." His oversized lips sagged sadly. "Don't look like they'd treat a boy that way—them over there in Thailand or Hong Kong or somewhere."

Or he would tell about Sara Jane: "Poor little thing's heart skipped a beat or two this morning and scared her helpers half to death." Or: "Little ol' girl asked me to give you this," and would slip me a piece of hard peppermint candy to melt in my mouth.

"It sure was rowdy in the chil'ren's ward today," he said one evening. "They all upset about Nurse Lucy takin' some of 'em's privileges away."

"What'd they do?" I asked.

"She caught one of them little 'uns with some pictures of naked ladies. You know how they are."

I figured Lanier was probably sharing with them the erotic evils of pornography, which they all craved.

"I told Lanier he better watch hisself," he said, half in jest.

Two technicians visited my room every day. They cut a sliver out of the left side of my cast. They applied a vise-like contraption which they screwed outward, little by little, every morning. In this manner, Dr. Braswell explained, they would twist my body within the cast until my spine was as straight as they could force it. After they widened the hole every morning, they rolled me to x-ray every afternoon. They took pictures of my back from different angles: shifting in one direction, demanding that I hold that awkward position, then turning me over and stating that I should not move, then another and another. Every afternoon, these sessions became longer and longer, more and more exasperating, more and more painful.

By the time they took me back to my room I was totally exhausted.

I lay in my twisted position, looking up at the spider. I
watched the spider working without regarding me even once,
concentrating on the job at hand, spinning her web, dancing
about upside-down on her tiny crooked black legs.

Watching her work, I fell asleep and awakened to the smell of
supper from the large ward room.

The spider never slowed her pace.

She worked without consideration of my situation. She could
care less if I was suffering. She didn't give one iota of thought
to my agony. She never stopped long enough to rare back on her
haunches and regard me with some degree of contemplation.
Her long legs just kept pumping away, working back and forth,
back and forth.

The sounds of the children's ward became more real now: the
constant pump-and-wheeze of Sara Jane's iron lung, the rambling voices on the far sides of the curtains, the whines, the
moans, the cries in the middle of the night, the humdrum sound
of the heaters pumping up steam through the system when the
temperature dropped outside, the droning of televisions set at
different channels throughout the central hallway, nurses talking
medical talk or gossiping, and the quick footsteps of doctors in
the hallway. I always knew when a doctor was approaching.
Doctors always walked twice as fast as anyone else. Visitors
dragged their feet reluctantly. Families plodded with heavy,
hard, doleful footfalls.

T e n

One evening after dinner, I overheard Dr. Braswell telling Mama and Daddy in the hallway outside my room that my surgery was scheduled for day after tomorrow. Tired, I closed my eyes. The surgeon had cut a rectangle-shaped door in the back of my shell and had fixed it with adhesive hinges. Each day when he entered, I was rolled onto my side, lifting my head into the air while he probed my tender back with the tips of his fingers.

I prayed a lot the next two days. I remembered, "The Lord is my shepherd and I shall not want . . ." and repeated it to myself. George Washington said that he and his wife, Louella, and all their children were praying for me. "I know you'll do just fine," George said, and he grasped my hand and held it snugly and warmly.

Brother Will came down from our church in Tuscaloosa. When he came through the door I saw his face change with sudden recognition of the pain and ugliness that he beheld. My hair had grown long and shaggy, although Daddy had clipped it back at the ends. There was no way to keep it groomed within the cast. It appeared unkempt at best. And I knew that I smelled. I could smell myself: the perspiration, the semen I excreted every time I read *The Story of O* or gazed into the photographs in *Playboy*, the ointment that anointed my poor, wrecked body. Even Brother Will in all of his reverent glory could not escape the pitiful sight of his parishioner twisted as no human being should be twisted, living in a world of pain, about to undergo torture like no human being should be asked to endure. Brother Will and Mama and I held hands while he said a prayer, thanking the Lord for everything that He had done for us and asking Him to be with me in my time of great physical discomfort.

On the night before surgery, Lanier rolled his chair to my side. He said that Sara Jane Matthews wanted him to kiss me for her. I laughed and said that wasn't necessary.

"Tell her I'll be picturing her in my mind in the moments before the anesthetics begin working," I said.

Lanier, shifting smartly in his wheelchair, glanced toward the door.

He squeezed the chair closer to my bed and leaned to me. In a whisper, he said, "Sara Jane asked me to deliver a special message."

I wormed to the edge, listening attentively.

"She said to tell you . . ." He cleared his throat.

I waited.

"She said when you are able to walk again, she wants you to come to her behind the curtains. I will stand watch while she makes love to you." With half-closed eyes, Lanier scrunched his large dramatic face. "She said that she would do it—'with fearful trust.' " He raised his thick black eyebrows, his swarthy forehead creasing. "Do you realize what she means?"

Without embarrassment, I said, "Yes."

"She wants to make love to you the only way she can."

"Tell her . . ." My voice halted. "Tell her that I will come."

He almost laughed, but he didn't.

"I mean . . ."

"I know what you mean." He reached out and touched my cast just beneath my chin. "Take care."

He wheeled around and marched out of my room. I knew that he was going directly to Sara Jane, where he would tell her what I'd said.

Nurse Elizabeth gave me three pills after only a swallow of water for supper and I slept until a medical team entered my room the next morning and started their work.

The door in my cast opened. I smelled an alcohol-based mixture being swabbed onto my skin. They spoke their medical words, succinct and precise. A new doctor brought plastic tubes followed by a nurse with a rolling cylinder. He attached one end of the tubes to the cylinder, brought the largest tube to my head, and explained the procedure. I opened my mouth. He sprayed dreadful gaseous fumes down my throat. I gagged, choked, then felt my throat grow numb. Within seconds, he rammed the tube past the place where my tonsils had once been. I gagged again. He shoved with more force. Another tube was fed up my nose. A moment later, he said, "Count back from a hundred."

"Ninety-eight, ninety-seven, ninety-six . . ."

I watched from atop a gray metal cabinet high in the corner of a very bright room in the center of which my body was lying face-down on a table with a half-dozen people wearing mint-green jackets and white masks standing around me. All were bent forward. A pump sounded rhythmically, followed by a sucking sound. For a moment I thought they'd attached Sara Jane's iron lung to my cast. Then I saw another square metal box sitting near my head. Tubes and wires were attached to it. The doctor who'd told me to start counting sat on a stool facing my head. He looked from the open door in the back of my cast to the metal box that flashed numbers on a panel. Dr. Braswell stood on one side of me. His fingers were buried in my blood and bones, working at my spine like the spider at her web, fastening, twisting, turning, pulling, his elbows bent out like wings, his fingers moving, weaving a strand of colorless pliable gristle, lowering and fastening, tying a knot, pulling upward again, the same way I'd seen Nanny at work at her sewing machine.

From my perch I saw a nurse lean over my body and wipe sweat from Dr. Braswell's brow. Another nurse handed him a pair of long-nosed pliers he used to turn something in my back, stretching it to the far side, then back again.

The man in front of my head reached out and turned knobs on the metal box. As he turned, the box made a high-pitched siren sound, louder and louder, faster and faster. From another machine, rapid beeps sounded in no perceptible rhythm.

Dr. Braswell glanced up.

"The oxygen," the counting doctor said.

"I can't stop now," Dr. Braswell said.

"No reason to," the other said.

Another doctor rounded the others and grabbed the blinking box and began turning other knobs and raising a lever.

The pumping machine stopped.

The siren whirred louder.

Another technician squatted next to the machine and turned two knobs frantically.

The man sitting in front of my head worked with knobs on his panel.

In less than a minute, silence fell over the room like an invisible blanket. The people continued to move but without the rhythm and the noise of the machines. Dr. Braswell sweated profusely and the nurse next to him wiped his forehead. Then the pumping machine started wheezing again.

The man in front of my head took a deep breath and said, "I was scared. For a minute, we'd lost him."

In the quietness of my room, I awakened with white-hot pain shooting through my body. I screamed. It hurt so bad, a pain twisted my backbone and made my head burst. It hurt so bad, I could not see even the tiles on the ceiling or the spider working. It hurt so bad, I was in a blind darkness.

Somewhere, I heard my father, "I don't give a damn what the doctor ordered, if you don't get him something to stop his pain, I'm gonna start throwing nurses out the window. You understand?"

His voice pierced the agony shrouding my brain. "Dammit, I said get the boy something! And I mean now!" in his most demanding voice.

In the hallway outside my room, he cursed. Mama said, "Oh, Harold, you don't have to—"

And he cut her off, saying, "I do have to, Myrtie. He's our son, and I'll be God damn if I'm gonna stand here and watch him in such pain. I have to do something. And they better do something—now!"

After a while, a doctor appeared at my side with a long syringe he slid into the skin of my biceps where puncture marks were already black and blue, splotched with hard knots. I closed my eyes. As he wiped the spot, he said, "It should take effect immediately."

Daddy's tobacco-heavy wheeze sounded near the foot of the bed. Breathing hard, angry and red-faced, he stared at me helplessly. I tried to smile. He touched my leg. "You'll be all right, Son," he said. He reached up and took the football from the shelf and squeezed it against his chest, his palms against the pointed ends, pushing them together unsuccessfully.

I closed my eyes and floated away.

I awakened as I had earlier, trying to shift my body within the cast, trying to escape my prison. Again, pain gripped my backbone and squeezed like a pair of pliers clamping down on spot after spot after spot, until they all blended together in one flaming mass of pain.

An electric shock careened through my limbs. I screamed as loud as I could cry.

Somewhere beyond the room, Daddy was cussing again. A nurse told him she had to wait another hour. In the distance, I heard him dialing and shouting into the phone, "Get your ass up to the sixth floor now, or I'm gonna give the boy a shot myself. Do you understand?"

Another doctor came and another needle pierced the muscle. Soon I drifted again into my Technicolored fantasy with Lanier Thompkins and Sara Jane Matthews. Lanier was not in a wheelchair and Sara Jane was dancing with long Cyd Charisse legs. We were a trio of lighter-than-air performers, beautiful with great bodies, twirling in the pink glow of twilight, energy building with each turn, arms outstretched, completely confident of our balance, tips of our fingers barely touching, sinewy, elegant muscles stretching long and fine, our pointed toes skimming the polished floor. Laughing, we could go on forever, our muscles moving with the sounds of violins, renewing our vigor as we floated like swirling ballet dancers in a ballroom surrounded by faceless admirers, waltzing on clouds.

I awakened in the middle of the night. The surgeon's scalpel slid between the vertebrae of my lower spine, twisted, and ripped away the red meat that I had seen from my perch in the operating room. But I was not anesthetized. I was wide awake, enduring the unbearable pain, writhing and moaning, biting my tongue and screaming.

Daddy pounded a desk in the hallway. Once again he demanded that I be given something to disguise the pain. "I don't give a damn what you need. I am only interested in my boy's welfare—not some miserable excuse you come up with to keep from doing your job. My boy's welfare!" he repeated. "Is that understood? Do I need to say it any plainer? I am tired of arguing with you people every time my son awakens and cries out. He is in horrible pain! I am tired, and I'm not going to simply talk next time. Do you understand?"

They must have understood. The next time I awakened screaming, a nurse stepped to my bedside, a hypodermic poised.

Four or five days after the surgery I could make it through the four hours between shots, withstanding whatever pain stabbed through my body, and I was fed solid food, which I regurgitated.

George Washington lifted me and held me with the muscles of his arms and his shoulders straining, mountains of muscles ribbing against his black skin, his eyes watching me closely. "You feel better?" he asked.

It was the first time since the surgery that at least some part of my body was not pressing against the incision. He held me suspended for what seemed like a long, long time or no more than a minute. When he finally lowered me to the bed, holding me as gently as he would a tiny baby, the pain stabbed, then subsided.

"I'll do you like that eight or ten times a day, long as you want me to," he said. "Maybe it'll take some of the hurt away."

"Thank you," I said, grabbing his arm where the muscles still jerked, like heavy taut ropes beneath the skin, and I closed my eyes and drifted again into the dreamworld.

Lanier Thompkins wheeled to my side and said Sara Jane wanted me to know that she was suffering with me. "When we hear your cries, we all hurt," Lanier said dramatically, his big head tilted.

"Tell all the people on the ward I'm okay," I said. "After a while, I'll be fine. Tell Sara Jane that I dreamed about her: a beautiful morphine dream."

Lanier said, "They're the best kind. She knows."

I watched the spider working on its magnificent, multi-layered web that now stretched a full twelve inches across the corner, drooping delicately, swaying downward. Late one afternoon the far corner broke and swung down. The spider rushed across the ceiling. Careful in her footing, she danced, snatching the loose end and stretching it back to its original position. She scrambled, weaving a knot. She tied it securely, giving the end an extra twist before she backed away and sat and examined the product of her handiwork. Satisfied, she moved again to the place where she had been working when interrupted.

The following week I was again prepped for surgery. Mama and Daddy returned. Donnie Lee, whose ten-year-old face was round as a saucer, came and stood next to my bed. I held his hand when his frightened eyes wondered over my odd-shaped body covered by the mountain of plaster. I knew that no matter how detailed Mama's explanation might have been, it was nothing like the view that he saw when he came through my doorway.

My shell had aged. Blood-blackened streaks rippled down the side. The cup beneath my chin had yellowed through my various sicknesses. Quarter-moons beneath my arms had turned brownish gray and smelled like a turtle who'd lain too long in the sun on a west Alabama blacktop.

"If you think this looks awful," I whispered to Donnie Lee, "you ought to see down there around my pecker, where I've peed and Lord only knows what else." He flashed a round freckle-faced smile.

Daddy told me he was already planning my homecoming, when I would be transported to Tuscaloosa in an ambulance. "They'll turn on the siren out on Hargrove Road, where everybody in the neighborhood can hear you coming," he said proudly.

I didn't tell him I didn't want a party. I didn't want people seeing me in this putrid shell. I didn't want them coming and gazing at the freak. I didn't want them smelling me and shaking their heads and muttering, "Poor kid." But you didn't tell Daddy things like that. It only made things worse. I kept quiet.

George Washington came and picked me up again and held me steady.

The next morning I went through the process again, feeling the lightness creep over me as I started counting down from one hundred and not making it to ninety-six, drifting off into a world apart.

This time I did not watch from atop the cabinet. I awakened with the pain. Daddy shouted. Nurses and orderlies reacted. I dreamed about Lanier and Sara Jane, and we were once again beautiful dancers, defying gravity, loose and free, dancing to the music of a quartet of violins.

A week later the medical people began weaning me off the narcotics. I fought the withdrawal pain. Daddy pitched a fit, but in the hallway outside my room Dr. Braswell told him, "Shut up, Mr. Morgan, and listen to me." Daddy hushed while the surgeon told him I was medically addicted to morphine. I had to be taken off the drug before I could be released for home care. Daddy spat several words, then marched away in defiance.

I struggled. The pain of withdrawal was as bad as the physical torture. The nurses gave me a substitute for morphine. My body reacted, my hands shaking, my head quivering in the confines of the cast, my muscles tensing, relaxing, then tensing again. After a very long thirty-some hours, while Lanier came to me and talked softly and said Sara Jane was still waiting, sweat poured from my forehead, my neck and my body. George Washington stayed with me through the night. He wiped my face with a cold rag. He threw aside the blanket and the sheet and rubbed my exposed legs with alcohol. He bathed my arms in coolness, washing them with alcohol and massaging whatever muscle remained on the bone. My eyelids grew heavy and finally closed, and I slept, a deep, sound, heavy sleep.

When I awoke, I was completely refreshed. The nurses washed me again as George had the night before. When they finished, the nurses said I would be going home soon.

Late that day George came to me. He washed me again with alcohol. Then he spread oil on my flaky dry skin. He rubbed it, again massaging the muscles that had grown useless with inactivity.

Eleven

The ambulance sped down the highway toward Tuscaloosa. I was propped up so that I could peer out the back window at the forest disappearing behind us.

As Daddy had promised, when we hit Hargrove Road, the driver turned on the siren. The high-pitched scream resounded through my ears, echoing over and over. He kept it on as we turned into Cedarwood and onto Magnolia Avenue. When we stopped in our driveway, the siren stopped. But it continued to ring in my head, loud and shrill. Donnie Lee appeared in the rear window of the ambulance. He smiled, wide-eyed and round-faced, then he was surrounded by the entire Boy Scout troop, all of them gazing at me the way they'd stare at the fanged geek at the carnival, amazed and slightly afraid and not wanting to touch. With them was our leader, Aaron Brianlevel, whose face still held the I-told-you-so expression I had witnessed nearly a year ago when he originally discovered my physical disorder.

I picked Jake Sims out of the group and smiled into his thin-cheeked face. He was looking at me with more concern than the others. He looked as though he wanted to turn and run away. He didn't want to face my predicament. But I put out my hand and he moved out of the crowd and took my fingers in his, feeling that I was more alive than I first appeared.

All of them followed, like a parade, as the attendants lifted me and carried me into the house, through the living room and hallway into Mama and Daddy's rear corner bedroom, where they had installed a hospital bed and a television set extending from the ceiling just like the one in the hospital room I'd vacated little more than an hour ago.

After Mama fluffed a pillow under the shell beneath my head, Donnie Lee, the boys, and Mr. Brainlevel moved near my bed. Daddy appeared through the doorway wearing his all-black cowboy outfit: boots, spurs, and a wide-brimmed hat. Years ago, Donnie Lee and I had made the mistake of telling him our all-time favorite western hero was Lash LaRue. Since then, on special occasions, he dressed up and showed off his skills.

As he jingled across the floor, unsnapped the leather whip and let it out the length of the room, I uttered, "Oh, no," and Mama glanced my way, feeling the sudden exasperation Daddy often evoked.

Daddy grabbed Jake by the arm and pulled him from the group and instructed him to stand next to the tall chest of drawers with a folded piece of paper poking from his clinched teeth. "Hold your hands straight down your sides," Daddy directed, as Jake straightened his back against the piece of furniture. The paper jiggled nervously in Jake's mouth while Daddy pulled the whip back, letting it slither across the floor.

As Daddy cocked his wrist and prepared to snap the whip, Mama hissed, "Harold, pleeeassse!" her voice snapping between her thin lips.

Daddy glanced toward her as though she had just grabbed him and shaken him awake. As quickly as he had entered, the cowhide handle slid from his fingers and fell with a thud to the floor. He pulled himself upright and straightened his shoulders. He turned on his heels and stepped away, passing between Mama and Mr. Brainlevel, looking at neither.

All of the Scouts filed out. They glanced toward me with forced, uncertain smiles and nods. Jake hesitated next to the bed and said he'd see me in a few days.

After the incident as Lash LaRue, Daddy stayed gone all afternoon and into the night. I heard the backdoor slam and waited for their voices to rise, but all I heard was muffled sounds from the kitchen. After a while, Daddy's face, flushed and needing a shave, appeared at the open door to the bedroom. "You awake, sport?" he asked.

"Yes, sir," I said.

He entered. He was now dressed his usual way: a shirt with a nondescript tie and creased gaberdine trousers. Daddy always wore a tie, unless we were going on vacation. His hair was slicked back and his eyes were glistening damply.

"How's the first day home?" he asked as he moved to my bedside.

"Okay," I said.

He looked around the room. "You got everything you need?" he asked. The sharp sweet fragrance of alcohol tinged his breath. Tiny red lines mapped his eyes. He smiled through a misty haze.

"I've got everything," I said.

"Still got the *Playboy*?"

"I left it with the kids at the hospital."

"Well, now isn't that charitable." I couldn't tell if he was serious or making fun of me.

He stood next to the bed and looked like he didn't know what to do with his hands.

"You want me to find another one?" he asked.

"Well . . ."

"I'll look."

"Okay."

He looked the length of the bed, then back up to my head.

"Is there anything I can do for you?" he asked.

"No, sir," I said.

"Well, if you can think of anything, just holler. Okay?"

"Yes, sir."

The ceiling of my room was a square milk lake, flat, without a ripple, clean, without inhabitants. I stared into it until my eyes hurt. A pain grew from directly behind my eyes, sliding down into my body, down my twisted reinforced backbone, into my middle where it spread before splitting down each of my thighs.

Hearing Mama and Daddy and Granddaddy and Nanny somewhere in the house, their voices muted with a kind of reverence for my presence, I felt suddenly as alone as I'd ever felt, like I was invading their territory, like I was a stranger from a faraway land. It was even worse than that first moment Mama and Daddy left me in the hospital room.

I stared into the ceiling, seeing nothing.

Time ticked slowly. Each second clicked in my brain. Instead of counting holes in the ceiling, I counted the ticks of the clock. Sixty in a minute. Three-thousand six-hundred in an hour. My brain expanded with emptiness.

Lying there, staring into nothingness, I felt a presence, looked toward the door, saw Mama's face framed in sadness, questioning. I gazed into her blinking eyes. She tried to smile.

"What's wrong, darling?" she asked softly.

"What's wrong?!" My voice broke.

Mama stepped into the room.

"I'm here, that's what's wrong," I stated flatly.

"Honey," she said. Her voice sounded empty. She reached toward me, touched my naked leg.

I pulled away. "Don't!" I snapped.

"Thomas?"

I glared toward her.

Tears welled in her eyes.

"Don't!" I said again, the sharp staccato sound edged in anger.

"Thomas," she said again. "I wish . . ." Her voice broke and halted.

I tried to turn away but the cast stopped me, held me, too heavy and bulky and awkward, too ugly and stinking. I closed my eyes, wishing I could escape this world, wanting to float up out of the cast, thinking that I could sprout wings and fly.

"I wish you didn't have to do this," Mama said.

"I'm a goddamn prisoner," I said.

"Thomas!"

"Well, I am," I said. "I'm a prisoner. I can't even move. I'm captured in some damn doctor's torture chamber." My words were my weapon, something sharp to wield.

"I wish I could change places with you," she said. Tears washed down her cheeks.

"Well, you can't," I said.

She touched my arm. She let her hand rest against my skin. Her fingers patted my forearm.

I lay back and closed my eyes. I tried to imagine I was somewhere else. I thought about the beach at Panama City: white sand stretching as far as I could see, the blue-green water lapping onto the sand, washing it with smelly, salty foam. Donnie Lee and I ran giggling, jumping into the shallow water that washed away our footprints in the sand. It was another world, and I was there, until I heard Mama say, "Can I get you anything?"

In the days ahead I watched a lot of television. It was mostly stupid and mundane. Nanny and Granddaddy sat with me in the morning for the *Arthur Godfrey Show*. Granddaddy believed Arthur Godfrey was the finest and most talented man in the country. In the evenings we watched *Talent Scouts* or a western movie or *Sky King*. On Sunday we looked at Ed Sullivan and his guests, which always included a juggler and a ventriloquist. Watching, I thought that in my cast I would make a perfect ventriloquist's dummy.

Granddaddy brought me his latest invention. He had brought some tools down from the farm in Samantha community and had designed and built a bookstand to fit snugly on each side of my shoulders, holding a book upside-down about ten inches above my eyes with springs fitted onto the top and bottom in order that I might adjust it to any size. He also arranged a light behind my head that I could flip on with the snap of my thumb. None of these actually worked. The leaves of the book kept falling. The light cast shadows onto the unsteady book. But I did not complain. Granddaddy had worked hard in his attempt to please me.

Every time I tried to read, the pages slid down and floated above my face. It became too much of an effort and I lacked the patience or the ability to concentrate. Television was easier.

Granddaddy had made a scratching stick from a coathanger. He fixed a piece of foam rubber to the end, wrapping it with twine. When a spot on my side itched, I rammed the wire down until I found the spot, then I'd rub it back and forth, around and around.

Nanny made some chicken and dumplings, and Mama fed me bite by bite, and they were the best-tasting stuff I'd eaten in months.

Two weeks after I got home Jake Sims came back. After Mama left him in my bedroom, he shifted around the end of the bed, sort of circling me slowly, barely touching, looking at me from all angles, the same way the spider had regarded me from the ceiling of the hospital room. "I'm a helluva sight, ain't I?" I said.

He shrugged.

"Well, I'm not something you want to look at every day, I'll tell you that," I said. "And I smell pretty bad too."

"Like roadkill." He grinned.

"I'd be good company for a buzzard," I said, grinning.

He gazed at the gray-green-brown-stained cast that encased my head from my chin around my ears and up to the crown. "Does it hurt?" he asked.

"It ain't comfortable."

"How do you . . .? You know?" He made a face and gestured toward my middle.

"Piss and shit?"

"Yeah."

"There's holes down there."

He shrugged.

"Somebody has to bring a pan."

He made another face.

"You have to do what you have to do," I said.

"Yeah, but . . ."

He came back only two more times.

I figured we'd see each other enough when I got out of the cast.

Daddy never stayed a whole week on the road. He came home after two or three days, sometimes driving too far. When he came in he'd come directly to my room. "I met an interesting old man in Eutaw the other day," he said. In a rush of words he would tell me about a fortune teller in Opp or a Greek he'd met in Fayette traveling the world in a hot-air balloon or a Ku Klux Klan Grand Wizard he'd heard speak in a field on the edge of Columbus, Mississippi. "That man spouted some of the meanest words I've ever heard in all my life," Daddy said. When I asked why he went to hear him, he said, "I always want to know what Jesus or the devil has to say." His eyes broadened. "If you don't listen to all sides, you'll never know what to believe and what to be against. That Grand Wizard preached hate. His words stung with a fire that'd burn pure hell in a soft and sweet place. If I didn't listen to him, I'd never know that that kind of hellfire existed on earth. If I just listened to sweet folks, like you and your Mama, I'd never know how to judge the other side."

Once he told about a midget he'd run into at a boardinghouse in Frisco City and said, "You know, that boy was talking poetry ninety-to-nothing. Pretty words that described a hillside full of fire and light on the shores of the Gulf down in old Mexico. It was a hillside where bright red poinsettias grew wild and thick as a carpet. If you didn't listen to that boy all dressed up frilly and fine with lace around his collar and knicker-style britches, you'd probably think he was some kind of sissy. But, Son, it doesn't matter how somebody dresses or how he's got his hair done up. If he's got poetry in his bones, you'll know it by his words and his actions. That's enough."

T w e l v e

After six weeks at home, my body healing, the ambulance returned and took me back to Birmingham. The same technician who had put the cast on my body took it off. A whirring electrical saw cut away piece by piece. Feeling the heat of the saw cutting near my skin, I tensed and waited. With the jerk of a knife, the piece ripped away and fell to the floor. I relaxed, waiting for the next. Finally, as the last piece dropped, I lay frightened, wondering what would happen next.

I waited while another technician began his work. After a nurse swabbed my stomach and back with an alcohol substance, making it sting and tingle, the man began wrapping pieces of cloth soaked with the plaster not unlike the cast that had first been placed on my body. This one stopped at the waist and fit across my right shoulder.

"It'll be dry by tonight," he said, then he warned me not to try standing by myself. "You'll need help, until you learn to walk again."

When I was rolled to the room on the sixth floor, the parts of my body now free of the larger cast felt light as air. The air next to my left thigh and around my neck and head was cool and refreshing—scary and unnatural. I shivered.

In my room, I lay waiting, my muscles weakened, my bones stiff. I gazed up into the corner. I squinted and looked closer. There was not even a sign of the spider's web.

I pushed my buzzer. A strange orderly answered my call. "Is George Washington around?" I asked.

"No, sir," he said. "He's off today."

I frowned. I'd thought George would be here. I had been looking forward to seeing him.

"Is this the same room where I was before?" I asked.

The man nodded. "Yes, sir, this is it," he said.

I looked again into the far corner. The spider's web had disappeared.

I lay in the bed thinking that any minute Lanier Thompson would roll himself down the hallway to greet me. Feeling a heavy loneliness, I closed my eyes and drifted into sleep.

I awakened with a big, round, black face with round, brown, red-lined eyes peering down at me.

"George?"

"How you doing, my man?" His voice sang.

I managed a smile. "I'm doing good, George." I reached out to him and he took my hands and squeezed warmly. "I was hoping you'd be here, George. I missed you."

"And me you," he said.

I blinked to hold back the tears that tried to seep from behind my eyes.

"You looking good," he said.

"I've been kinda chilled," I said.

"Here, let me get you some covers," he said, moving quickly around the bed to the closet from which he extracted a blanket that he spread over me like he had done months ago. He pulled an end of the blanket up to my chin. "That better?" he asked.

I smiled and nodded. The back of my neck ached. I reached around and could actually feel the skin between my head and my back.

"Let me rub you and fix you up," George said. Before I could say another word, he pulled open a drawer and took out several bottles. He poured alcohol over my thigh and hip and around my neck, making it sting with the first touch. Then, touching gently, like he was working with priceless porcelain, he moved his fingers in slow, swirling motions, spreading the liquid, making my skin tingle with life.

At several spots he stopped, uttered a pained grunt, took another liquid from another bottle, and said, "This gonna burn," as he dipped a ball of cotton into the orange mixture and lifted it with a pair of long tweezers and touched it to the sore place. "That ol' cast rubbed you bad," he said. "Place here on your back's gotten infected." And again he swabbed with the cotton. It stung, but not for long. Then he rolled me once again, gently, onto my back. "You're gonna be fine," he declared.

After a while, I said, "George, I haven't seen Lanier. I thought he'd be waiting for me."

George swallowed hard. "Lanier's been released. He went home several weeks ago."

"He's doing better?"

George shrugged and looked away. "Not much better, to tell the truth."

"So, why'd they . . ."

"The doctors say they've done all they can for him. They gave him some medication. I think it helps with the pain. His mama and daddy came back from wherever they've been and fixed up a room out behind their house. They've got round-the-clock help. Offered me a job, but I told 'em I was happy right here."

"You mind rolling me into the ward room?" I asked.

He found my robe in the closet, fitted it around my shoulders, then he leaned down and put his long arm around my body and lifted me. He lowered me slowly.

When my feet touched the floor it was like a hundred needles sticking into the bottoms. Tiny bolts of pain shot up my legs. My ankles buckled, but George kept me balanced as he slid me into the wheelchair.

"You'll be walking in no time," he commented.

"I'll have to learn all over again," I said. "Like when I was a baby."

"I know, but I'll help you this time."

He rolled me into the large room. The whole place seemed empty. There was more space than I remembered. It was filled with an overwhelming silence. When I listened I heard no rhythmical sucking and pumping. At the distant cubicle a curtain had been pulled back. The late afternoon sun shone through the bank of windows above the empty place where the iron lung had sat. I looked up into George's face.

In a husky voice, he whispered, "She passed a week ago," as if he were afraid that fully spoken words might disturb someone. "Poor little thing. That old machine just couldn't keep her going any longer."

I nodded. Suddenly I realized that I was surrounded by silence, and I knew the children's ward was never without sound. A breeze did not stir. Even the air seemed dead.

George started to turn the chair.

I raised my hand. "Let me sit here for a while," I said.

"Sure," he said. "You sit here long as you want." I heard his nearly imperceptible footfalls withdraw.

I sat in the empty place and felt the warmth of the sun through the windows. I lifted my hands from the arms of the chair. They trembled. When I tried to picture her, something obscured my vision. If I had gone to her and lowered my head onto hers . . . if I had put my lips to hers . . . it would have been a sweet little kiss. Just a little kiss.

After a while the silence and the dream vanished. The sound of children flickered unevenly behind the curtains at the far end of the large room. Someone called a name. The irregular beeps sounded from a machine somewhere in the maze of curtains. A child cried out.

Soon, I knew, I too would be leaving this place. Life, as complex and fragile as a spider's web, continued, pain endured. I would return to other hospitals like this one over and over again throughout my life. Each with its own shiny emptiness, each impersonal in its own way. We labored in our everyday existence just as the spider laboriously crocheted her path across the ceiling of my world. We planned without knowledge of what lay ahead. Each bend in the road gave the promise of surprise but no assurance of fulfillment. The promise was enough to keep us trudging forward, like a breeze across a meadow, people moving toward some unsure but inevitable future.

S t o r i e s

M y   O r i g i n a l   S i n

On the day she moved next door, Edna Williams was a sight
to behold.

I was thirteen, and like Daddy, I enjoyed looking at pretty
women, and Mrs. Williams was more than just pretty. There
was a mystery about her.

On a summer evening in June, Mama and Daddy sat on the
back porch. My brother, Donnie Lee, and I were catching lightning bugs in a fruit jar. In a half-whisper, Mama said, "I think
Edna Williams's kinda loose. Ralph's her third husband, and
she's not thirty yet." Mama's words in my mind, I took to walking past the Williams's window on the way to the paddock
where I kept Navaho, my pinto pony. I sneaked glances into the
private shadowy world of her bedroom. It was my first experience as a voyeur.

Sometimes I waited in the night, crouched under the shrubs
at the corner of our house. Once she slid out of her blouse,
wearing only a flesh-colored brassiere. As she stepped toward
the window my breath caught. She hesitated. Before she
reached the window, she turned away. I stepped out of hiding,
tripped, scrapped my knee against gravel, and scampered into
the house, feeling guilty.

Two weeks later I was walking my pony toward the stables. In
her back lawn she stood in the morning sunshine, hair glistening as though it had just been washed, arms lifting to a clothes-

line. The thin material of her housecoat stretched over her backside, showing the imprint of panties. My heart fluttered as I watched the hem climb up the backs of her thighs. After the clothespin snapped, she withdrew, dipped into her basket, then rose again to a brief moment of sexual tension.

Navaho nudged me while Edna Williams turned and gazed into my face, her look drifting from surprise to amusement, her lips parting. Smiling, she winked. I took a deep breath— my insides quivering—my stomach tightening. I gathered the reins in my sweaty palm and half-ran to the stables.

That night, I relived that solitary moment when she leaned to the clothesline. I felt a stirring and was sure that by tomorrow morning my penis would be covered with warts. Between preachings last winter at the Primitive Baptist Church, where Granddaddy and Nanny went every second Sunday, my freckle-faced first cousin, Billy Joe Hassell, warned that when boys got "impure thoughts" warts popped up all over "their thing." The remembered words brought a full-length view of Edna Williams without the flesh-colored brassiere, breasts full and round and white as a Christmas angel, pink-tipped, pointing at me, accusing. I rolled over and gripped the pillow and prayed.

When I awakened I sneaked to the window and peeped out around Roy Rogers curtains. A light shone in her empty bedroom. In the bathroom, I took hold of myself and examined every inch and found no sign of warts.

Although I walked Navaho under her window a dozen times, I did not see her. At night I pictured her panties tight against her behind, her taut thighs, her lazy blue-eyed look, her lips parting. I took hold of myself and prayed to God to allow me to exist without warts, although it seemed that impurity was quickly becoming my way of life.

On the first warm day after March, Ralph Williams mowed his lawn in a sleeveless undershirt. Sweat poured as he traversed the yard, and Daddy said that Donnie Lee and I should trim the shrubs. Working, I kept an eye out for Mrs. Williams, but she did not appear. That afternoon, as I was bringing Navaho in from our ride, a voice called, "Hi." She sat on their back steps watching her husband light charcoal in the grill. Her arms wrapped around bent legs, her thighs long and pale, naked to the edge of blue short-shorts.

She smiled, and old Ralph, with burned neck and slicked-down hair above his pale yellow wash-and-wear nylon shirt, looked up. "Your parents have gone to Little League with your brother," she called. "They said you could have hamburgers with us. You like hamburgers?"

"Ye . . . ye . . . yeah," I stammered. Then I kicked the pony and bounced down the lane.

When I returned she was sitting in a plastic chair with long legs crossed, absently swinging her right calf, working her muscles as though in calisthenics.

As she fetched a lemonade, I said hello again to Mr. Williams, who told me to call him Ralph. He had thick, broad shoulders layered with muscles, and his clean sleeveless undershirt was visible beneath the yellow wash-and-wear shirt. His beard was shadowy. His eyes were dark, and he smelled sickeningly sweet with Vitalis and bay rum.

She brought a tall glass, the right shoulder of her peasant's blouse slipping as she handed it to me.

Keeping my eyes peeled on her, I sipped noisily.

She sat again on the back steps, patted the spot next to her.

I sat fixated, and she, looking across the yard, casually slid her tongue across her painted lips while Ralph poked at the coals and finished his Coke.

Mrs. Williams asked how long I had been riding, and I told her Navaho was my first horse, a Christmas gift three years ago, and I enjoyed playing cowboys and Indians, especially when I could imagine I was Lash LaRue, and she said Lash LaRue was her favorite too. "He's very sexy, the way he wears all black, walks with that swagger and cracks his whip."

After Ralph fixed another Coke, drinking the second one faster than the first, he said, "You always liked old Lash, him with that whip, like a phallic symbol."

"Oh, Ralph," she said, a giggle in her throat. "Don't say that. Not with . . ." and she gestured. Whatever a phallic symbol was, it was something they didn't want me to know. I'd have to search Webster's later.

Edna went inside, leaving me with Ralph and his fourth Coke. He turned the meat and said he prided himself as the best hamburger cook in Tuscaloosa. Daddy had bragged about the same thing last summer.

As the sun fell and lightning bugs took flight, sizzling sounded from the kitchen. Edna brought a platter filled with toasted buns and catsup and mustard, lettuce and tomato, and a pile of French fries. We ate under the yellow outside light, and again I could smell Ralph's whiskey-sour breath mixed with sweat and Vitalis and bay rum. Edna said I was a fine young man. She smelled of Ivory soap and French fries.

Later at home, I found out that Donnie Lee's baseball team had lost. I answered questions about how I enjoyed supper.

Donnie Lee cussed under his breath and kicked a kitchen cabinet shut—mad at himself for making an error in the sixth inning and letting a run score. He took baseball seriously, seeing himself a nine-year-old miniature Yogi Berra. I sneaked into the living room to the dictionary, flipped to "fallic," then changed the *f* to *ph* to discover it meant "human male organ," thinking that Lash LaRue's whip was surely one mighty big penis.

That September my third-period math teacher was Miss Judy Phillips, a thirty-five-year-old who had ample hips and large breasts and wore tight skirts and tight bras. Between jotting algebra equations on the blackboard, she twisted and turned, fidgeted with her blouse, pulled on her stockings and squirmed. By the end of her class half the boys were holding books balanced in their laps.

I was glad fourth period was phys ed. Old man Lewkowski, a second-generation Pole from Chicago, had come south in the army after World War II with his wife, an Alabama girl. He was wider and thicker than Ralph Williams, and he had a large, round rock-hard belly. He strutted about the gym and dared us to hit his belly with closed fists. "Hit it," he challenged. I balled my fist and swung into him. My fist bounced, sounding like the thump of a ripe melon. "Sissy!" he hissed.

When weather permitted, all of the boys ran around the block. The sweat washing down my tee shirt—cleansing all the impurities that had welled up during Miss Phillips's class. When we rushed naked into the showers, old man Lewkowski screamed, "You're all a bunch of sissies. Keep playing with your little ding-dongs and they're gonna fall off in your hands. If you play with yourself, you'll have ape hands." When I asked what ape hands were, he growled, "Hair'll grow between your fingers and cover your palm," and when we looked down, Coach Lewkowski laughed wildly, filling the locker room, his big belly shaking.

School let out for Christmas and I renewed my daily routine with Navaho. We rode past the Williams's bedroom window on the way out and when we came back home. I saw her a time or two, but she was always dressed in a suit or slacks.

One evening Navaho was huffing cold smoky breath when suddenly the Williams front door flew open and Edna rushed out into the night, slamming the door.

Halfway to the street, she stopped and looked back, her face puffy, her eyes red and wet, tears streaking her swollen cheeks. Looking at me, she mouthed, "Thomas."

"Mrs. Will . . ."

I threw my right leg over the horn and slid down. My booted feet plopped onto the cold damp earth as she reached me and grabbed my shoulders, like a sinking swimmer grasping a float. "Thomas," she said again, a desperate cry, and for a moment I thought she would hug me. But she stopped, holding me at arm's length.

Navaho pushed her nose against my shoulder, blowing her foggy breath and making a throaty sound. Edna Williams laughed through her tears, put out her hand and rubbed the horse's nose.

"Can I . . ." she started, then the front door swung open. From inside, where the Christmas tree lights blinked, Ralph Williams shouted, "Edna, get your ass back in here."

I started to say something, but she shivered, turned, moved toward the house and stepped inside, the door slamming shut again.

Navaho and I stood still. Through the front windows I tried to see beyond the cheerful decorations. I saw nothing but dancing shadows and heard muffled, angry sounds.

A half-hour later, after I'd rubbed Navaho down, I looked again, but the lights were off. The house was silent. In the distance I heard caroling somewhere in the neighborhood.

The night of my fourteenth birthday Edna left him. They had a fight, Daddy said. I detected a lilt in his voice, happy for another man's troubles. I had seen Daddy's downcast eyes seek solace after Mama turned away in disgust from one of his bad jokes. I had judged that Mama was usually right, and I knew that Edna Williams had every right to walk away from Ralph, who in my estimation was no better than Daddy.

The next morning, a Saturday, I took Navaho out. It was a gorgeous February day, a breeze barely blowing through skeleton trees, the sun bright and clear in the azure sky. Ralph Williams sat on his back steps holding a glass. He raised it. "CC and Coke, breakfast of champions," he announced, trying to smile. Then, as an afterthought, he uttered, "I wish to God she'd come back." Exactly ten years later, on the morning after my twenty-fourth birthday, when my wife walked out and left me with a Siamese cat named Zelda, I would realize the total loneliness and utter despair of drinking by myself at nine on a beautiful morning in February.

However, at fourteen, seeing Ralph Williams sitting with the drink in his hand, his eyes blood red, his stomach drooping, his hairy arms like an insect's appendages, I felt only repugnance and shame for him. I wanted to call Edna and tell her to stay where she was—she was better off without him.

But late that afternoon Ralph's prayers were answered. She rode up in a car that waited until Ralph bolted out and took her in his arms and kissed her while crying mumbled words of forgiveness.

I watched from the darkness beneath our corner shrubs, where I could escape the torment of my own parents who found life more and more unbearable—my mother making a good living as the assistant to the director of the new hospital and my father feeling the pressure when his work as a traveling salesman dropped off to nearly nothing. Each day into my fourteenth year I grew lonelier, my best friend in the world a pinto pony named Navaho, to whom I told everything.

I saw Edna less and less. Mama told Daddy that the Williams were trying to have a baby. Edna thought a baby would bring them closer, Mama said. My insides ached, picturing them growing closer and closer, until they rubbed together in my imagined vision. Daddy grumbled and shuffled to his car and roared away, facing another week of traveling, selling less and less.

Eighth grade was no better than the seventh. I caught the eye of Linda Lacey, a pretty strawberry blonde across the aisle in history. She smiled sweetly and raked her pencil off her desk, and I knelt and retrieved it, like one of Uncle Wheeler's bird dogs.

During mid-morning recess, Brother Field, the big-shot of our class, grabbed Linda Lacey's purse and ran with it. She squealed. Hearing her distress, I rushed to show my courage. When Brother whirled around a gigantic oak, I stepped in his path. He reached out and shoved me. Off-balance, I stumbled over an exposed root. Falling, I hit my elbow in the hard dirt but immediately scampered away, circling. As Brother ran, I climbed onto the concrete steps, crouched and waited. As Brother raced by, I leaped. I hit shoulder-high, knocking him into the dirt. The assistant principal, Mrs. Edwards, stepped out the front door and jerked me up. Before I could explain, she led me to the office and sat me down on a long wooden bench. I tried to talk but was ordered to sit in the rear corner of my classes for three weeks and stay after school for a week. After stay-in period, a boy named Jake Sims was waiting in the side yard. He had a little red Cushman motor scooter and offered a ride. "Sure," I said and climbed on. Talking against the wind as we rode east on Hargrove Road, Jake said, "I saw what that damned Brother Field did. He's a bully and an asshole." When we pulled up to my house, he said, "You want to get him back?"

We planned a scheme. At recess, Jake would challenge him, get his dander up, and I would pounce on him when he chased Jake around the corner. We were out of sight when we ambushed him. It all worked until Linda Lacey screamed that we were hurting Brother. Two teachers scurried out the door, nabbed me and Jake. Then we both had to wait for the principal and were both given after-school time. Every afternoon I rode home with Jake, and we became fast friends.

I never discovered why Linda screamed. I wanted to tell her off, but every time I got mad, I looked into her eyes and all my anger melted away.

At home, Mama became more confident. She was given a raise and was appointed the hospital director's executive assistant. Daddy stayed away more and more. Mama said his accounts were dwindling because he had a short fuse. Beauty shop operators didn't want him upsetting their customers and barbers didn't want him telling them how to run their businesses. Daddy flew off the handle, saying loudly that his temper was no worse than anyone else's. Donnie Lee went off to baseball practice while I hid in the shrubs and watched for Edna Williams.

I never told Mama about my detention. She heard from a doctor's wife whose daughter was in my class. She asked why I hadn't told her and I hung my head and murmured that I was ashamed. "Well, you should be," she snapped. In the center hallway Mama put her hands on my shoulders and we dropped to our knees. I prayed for her to hit me. I couldn't stand the weight of her hands gently upon my shoulders. Her words came, soft and furious, praying for the Lord to "wash away all the hatefulness that is filling this boy's heart." When she lifted her hands, I felt a cool forgiveness wash through my body. She ordered me to study alone in my room. I was grounded for three weekends.

Friday night, while I hung around the house, acting like I was watching TV while figuring out a way to escape and slip off with Jake Sims, Daddy came home and dropped his sample-case onto the floor and slumped into a chair at the kitchen table. Mama stood in front of the sink and glared at him. He did not look back. He stared into the empty glass he toyed in his fingers. After a while, she said, "Harold, you used to never drink." He said nothing. He raised his hand and slung the glass. It crashed against a cabinet three feet from Mama. He slid his chair back. He stood. His shoulders slumped and he muttered, "Bullshit," and turned and walked out the front door, slamming it.

I heard his car leave. I went out the back door. Mama called, "Where do you think you're going?" I said, "Outside." And she said, "Well, don't go far," her voice breaking.

I walked down the path. I glanced toward the Williams's window but saw only darkness. At the stable I rubbed Navaho's nose and told her I was sorry I hadn't ridden her in a long time, and she nuzzled her soft nose next to my cheek, and I wanted to cry, but I didn't.

I talked to Navaho about Linda Lacey and Brother Field, about my new friend Jake Sims, who didn't like horses, and even about Edna Williams and how breathtakingly beautiful and sensuous she was and how the simple memory of her smell was driving me to distraction. I scooped a handful of oats from the bin and held it out to Navaho—who Daddy sold at the end of the summer. He said I had lost all interest in the animal. I didn't protest.

By then, Jake Sims and I were drinking beer on Friday nights, bought for us by a tall black man who worked at the golf club where Daddy played gin-rummy on weekends. Sometimes Daddy didn't come home until after supper. When he did, Mama said little, stared at him and sniffed the air like a hound. Sometimes he didn't come home at all. Mama went to their room after supper and closed the door and whimpered until she began snoring.

Several times during the next year I heard the Williams's front door opening in the middle of the night. Ralph's footfalls sounded heavy on the sidewalk. His car door opened, then slammed. Like Daddy, he roared off, then I lay awake—picturing Edna alone in her bed.

During the fall of my sophomore year Jake Sims talked his older sister Gail into buying a fifth of Old Smuggler Scotch for us. Jake had read in Esquire that true gentlemen acquired a taste for Scotch, and we decided that we wanted to be true gentlemen.

Afraid that we might get into trouble on Jake's motor scooter, Gail said we should acquire our taste at her apartment. Her ex-husband, a long-distance truck driver, was on his way to Sacramento, and she didn't expect him for another week. "Y'all can buy some Seven-Up to mix with the Scotch," she said authoritatively, "and I'll fix steaks and baked potatoes," a sophisticated gourmet meal, like something out of a magazine, something a true gentleman might enjoy.

The first sip of Old Smuggler burned down my throat and hit my stomach like a liquid firecracker, exploding and bringing tears to my eyes. I blinked them clear, lifted my drink for a second try, watching Jake, who was sipping. My next swallow swirled around and settled heavy in a smoky cloud of uncertainty.

It was Indian summer—a warm and humid time after a few days of cool September air—and we all knew that soon the fall rains would begin and we'd pray for the downpour to stop. Stealing these few more days of summertime, Gail changed from her work dress to tee shirt and shorts. The thin shirt showed off her breasts and the shorts made the best of her stubby legs. After downing two more drinks, I did little to hide my obvious joy at seeing my buddy's sister's body.

Within an hour my taste for Scotch had been acquired. I was as sophisticated and suave as any gentleman in <u>Esquire</u>. I gazed longingly at Gail, whose feet curled under her bottom on the silver, crushed-velvet sofa beneath her four-by-six painting of a bullfighter in a glittering suit-of-lights on a background of black velvet. "Hey," I said and reached out playfully. "Hey, yourself," she said, and giggled as she took my fingers. "Guide me," she said, sliding down and tilting her face toward mine and parting her lips.

I was in heaven: drinking Scotch, listening to Gogi Grant singing "The Wayward Wind" and kissing the twenty-year-old divorced, sister of my best friend who was passed out on the living room rug.

As she slid her tongue between my lips, I groped for her breast. She moaned. She squirmed as I pushed her tee shirt up and unsnapped her bra. I lowered my face, and her fingers combed through my hair and clutched my head.

"Baby," she whispered urgently, raising her body. Her knees rose, parting, pushing, kneading my stomach that growled some animal-like sound as the smoke-flavored whiskey erupted. I rolled away, grabbing for the coffeetable, stumbling over Jake, nearly falling as I searched for the bathroom.

I crashed to my knees. I lowered my head, hugging the slick cold porcelain to my cheek. My lips opened as the liquid gushed up my throat and spewed into the bowl. "Awwww," I groaned. I spat and spat.

I closed my eyes. Somewhere music whirred. My stomach growled. A spasm gripped my middle.

A chill swept over my body, down through my shoulders to the tips of my toes. God was punishing me for all of my sinful ways, beginning with the first time I looked at Edna Williams.

Another spasm rushed through me. I wanted to cry out for Mama and for Daddy and for Edna Williams. When I looked up, blinded by the sudden light, Gail looked down and declared, "You poor baby." She took me by the shoulders and tried to pull me up.

I shook my head. "No," I said, "let me stay here." I reached around the commode and held tightly.

She released me and said, "I'll fix some eggs."

I shook my head again, then lowered my face.

She moved away. After my stomach shook several more times, I smelled something rancid cooking while the McGuire Sisters sang "Sincerely."

Gail came back and tried to lift me.

"Let me..." I started, pulling away.

"If you eat something, you'll feel better," she said.

I stared blankly, gazing into her red-rimmed eyes.

"Eat something, then you can sleep," she said. "I know."

I pulled myself up slowly. Finally I stood but did not move. I teetered. I reached out. I grabbed the sink. I held to it.

"Come on," she urged.

Shakily, I moved with her.

In the living room, Jake sat on the floor next to the coffeetable. He said something but I could not make out his words.

I shrugged.

"Come and eat something, and you'll feel a hundred-percent better," Gail promised.

I plopped down and stared at the plate filled with yellow scrambled eggs bordered by four triangles of golden toast.

The Four Aces sang, "Love is a Many Splendored Thing."

Gail poured a tall glass of cold milk.

I reached out. My fingers hit the glass.

"Watch it." She lurched for the glass.

I stared into her face and grinned. I took the glass in both hands and brought it shakily to my lips. The fresh milk washed over my parched lips, through my parched mouth and down my sore throat. It settled soothingly into my stomach.

I picked up a fork and began working at the eggs. After I finished the toast, I looked up at Gail and smiled at her.

"Want more?" she asked.

I shook my head.

Jake said he'd better go home. "Me too," I said, wondering if I would be able to climb into my bed and close my eyes and go to sleep and wake up and be assured that my world was safe, that it would be secure, that Mama and Daddy and Donnie Lee loved me and loved each other. I wished I had not allowed Daddy to sell Navaho. After a long nap I would take a long ride. I would talk to Navaho about all of this, and I would tell her how the world was changing too fast, too damned fast, and I could not slow it down, although I tried.

When Jake let me off, he shouted over the roar of the scooter's engine, "Take care. I'll see you at school Monday."

The house was quiet and peaceful, a pleasant place with gray asbestos siding, a green roof and well-trimmed shrubs under windows bordered by neat green shutters.

Halfway to the front door, I felt something erupt in my stomach. I ran toward my old hiding place at the corner of the house.

As I scooted under the shade of the low-lying branches of the evergreen bush, liquid and eggs spewed out. I leaned against the concrete-block foundation. I closed my eyes and prayed for forgiveness. Please, God...

I fell back and lay like a sorry drunken bum on my nest of last year's brown pine straw. With eyes closed, I heard Edna Williams's cry, "Nooo!" and knew that something terrible had happened. It was a primeval howl, lost in an unforgiving morning.

Hours later, after Mama found me asleep in my room where I had sneaked unnoticed, she sat on the corner of the bed and put her palm to my forehead and said, "You have a fever."

"I feel sick," I said.

In hushed, reverent words, Mama said that Ralph Williams had been driving back to Alabama from a sales meeting in Memphis early this morning. He was on the highway north of Fayette when a drunk driver came around a curve and swerved into his lane and hit him head-on. "All poor Ralph wanted was to get home in time for his and Edna's anniversary," she said. Then she whispered, "And poor Edna's pregnant."

I turned over, feeling miserable, and buried my face in the pillow.

Mama patted me softly on the shoulder. "Don't you worry about it, darling," she said.

She left me alone. I slept and dreamed. When I awakened I heard the steady drip-drop of rain. Later, I heard Edna Williams's lone voice again, wailing "No, God, nooo!"

That evening, as darkness crept slowly over our part of the world, I sat in my hiding place under the evergreen bushes smelling the fresh scent of the rain-washed earth. I gazed through the semi-darkness into the lighted window of her bedroom. Edna Williams stood next to a cream-colored wall and raised her arms. A man stepped toward her. Taller than she, he had to lean down for his mouth to fit onto her lips. His stance seemed familiar, the way he cocked his head when he looked into her eyes. I held my breath and wondered. When he pulled back, he held her head behind the neck under the sheen of blonde hair. I caught a glimpse but could not believe what I saw. I watched as they came together again. I closed my eyes and chased the thought from my brain. I waited and waited. Later, I awakened, alone, a steady drizzle drenching my clothes. The house was dark. The painful cry was memory. I felt my way through the shadows of our house. Outside the door to Mama and Daddy's bedroom, I listened. I waited. I heard Mama's light snore, then Daddy's heavy retort. I found my bed and lay down and closed my eyes.

When I was ten he was twenty years older, but we both saw the world in the same simplistic way. He was a chunky man, all round and soft with a giant's feet. When he grinned his face twisted into contortions, showing big yellow crooked teeth, and I laughed with delight at his antics. When his big fat face turned sad, full lips pouting, I wanted to reach out and hug him and make him know that I cared. His name was Dee, and he was my cousin.

He lived with his family down on the delta of the rivers that flowed into Mobile Bay in the wilderness of south Alabama. The three two-story frame houses of the family compound had wrap-around screened porches and several out-buildings for boats and other no-longer-used vehicles. The whole place was covered with huge broad-limbed live oaks, looking spooky, but great for climbing. Dee's mama and daddy, Aunt Lucille and Uncle Harry, lived in the middle house that was larger than the other two, where Cousin Sybil and her husband John and Cousin Ruth and her husband Kendall lived.

In the summertime, Dee and I sat on the screened porch of his parents' home and listened to the thousands of frogs and insects chirping in the woods. They made a wall of noise, and yet it was eerily quiet. Now and then the call of a lone bird drifted in from somewhere across the water, and Dee would shift his large, off-centered head sideways, scrunch his face, and say, "Whip-er-will," and I'd say, "Whippoorwill," and he'd nod and

say, "Whip-er-will, ol' Mockin'bird." At last light, we'd sit on the
end of the pier with our poles and drop hooks draped with
worms or crickets into the dark water alive with fish. By full
darkness we had a mess of perch that the colored boy Cater
helped us clean. When Dee and I grabbed the fish, they flopped
out of our grasp. Cater clamped their wiggly, slimey bodies
down on the boards next to the outdoor sink and held them
steady and cut around the gills and down the side. He took the
backside of a spoon between thumb and forefinger and raked
against the sides to scrap away the scales. Aunt Lucille floured
and fried the fish, fixed French-fried potatoes and cole slaw.
Sometimes she made hush-puppies as big around as my fists.
We'd sit on the back stoop where Cater helped with the feast,
eating off of yesterday's <u>Mobile Register</u>. None of the grown-
ups ever ate fish, although they went fishing out in the river, the
bay or the Gulf of Mexico every week or so. Sometimes they'd
dig up oysters and bring them back in croaker sacks, and Cater
would pry them open with his knife. I slurped them down without sauce, but Dee liked his swimming in catsup. He'd get red
stuff around his mouth and squirt a half-eaten oyster through
his teeth and Cater would frown and shake his head and I would
think if he kept doing it I would get sick.

Once I asked why we couldn't eat with the grown-ups in the
dining room the way Dee and I did at dinner on Sundays. Dee
scrunched his face into a heavy frown and said, "Cater can't eat
in there with us." And I said, "Oh," disappointed and unsure.
Later, after he'd thought about it for a while, Dee said, "Whites
don't eat with coloreds." When I got back home, I asked Mama
about it and she said, "Well, that's true in the South. In the
North, however, people don't discriminate." When I asked what
"discriminate" was, she said, "Up there, folks just look at one

another as folks," and I said that sounded like a good way to be. She smiled and kissed my cheek and said I was thinking right to think that way, but don't say it out loud too often, or I'd get into trouble. She always had a sweet way of explaining things.

The next summer Dee and I and Cater, who was twelve, built a canoe out of an old log from a tree that had blown down in a bad storm the past winter. "Ol' black bear lived in that tree," Cater said as we began chopping.

"Really?" I asked. The tree was located less than a half-mile up the red clay road from Aunt Lucille and Uncle Harry's place. I had never heard them talking about bears in these woods.

"There's bears all around," Dee agreed.

"Sure is," Cater said.

We cut through the sycamore log at two places fourteen-feet apart. Dee, who was strong as a young ox, lifted one end and heaved it to his shoulder. It took me and Cater to pick up the other end and balance it. Then the three of us toted it to a pair of sawhorses we had fixed in front of an out-building.

Then we started hewing out the inside, just like it showed in my Handbook for Boys I got as a Boy Scout. "This is the way the Indians did it," I explained to Dee, who couldn't read. "They'd travel miles and miles along the river in their dugouts."

"I heard Mr. Harry say you was the runt of the family," Cater said one hot afternoon while we were working. I glanced toward Dee, who was looking to see my reaction. "Well," I said, "I am the littlest one here," and both Cater and Dee chuckled and nodded. I'd never thought of myself as a "runt," although I was shorter than most. I figured, somewhere along the line, I'd have to prove just how big I was.

Cater was big for his age but not half as big as Dee.

We worked in the shade of the live oaks. From the long gracefully bowed limbs Spanish moss hung like decorations from long ago. When a breeze blew every afternoon before twilight, when the tides began to change in the Gulf to the south, the moss swayed gently. The loose gray strands rubbed together in the day's last breath, whispering undertones and warnings of night.

Cater rolled his eyes and gazed up through the trees into the gray sky. "Ol' ghosts talkin'," he said.

"Ain't no ghosts," Dee said. "Sybil and Ruth say they ain't no ghosts. John jokes. Kendall gonna spank him."

"There are no ghosts," I reassured him, but I looked around through the long shadows.

"Y'all don't know nothing," Cater said. "I been in ol' Nazareth Church when the ghosts of the dead come calling. They sing 'Amazing Grace' just like a long time ago. No music, no nothing, jus' voices."

"Oh, bullshit," I said.

"Don't cuss, Thomas Reed," Dee said.

"I'm sorry," I said. I had promised his mother I would never curse in front of him. She said she didn't want him learning bad habits. If he didn't hear me say it, she said, he would never say such things. "Dee's pure of mind," she said.

"You cuss, and I'll tell Mama."

"I won't," I promised.

"I tell you true," Cater said, his eyes big as half-dollars. "I was sittin' with Mama when a host of ghosts come down out of the heavens and sang the spiritual song."

"How do you know that?" Dee asked.

"I was sittin' right there on the pew," he said. "It made me want to hide my head in Mama's apron, I was so scared. Mama patted my knee and said for me to act like a big boy and not be scared, that it wasn't nothing but the heavenly hosts come call-in'." Cater shook his head. "I didn't hide, but I was scared slap down to my bones. I tell you that."

We kept to our work, but now and then we looked around to see if we saw something unusual. After the clouds swept over and the oaks whispered louder, we gave up and went to the porch, where Aunt Lucille said we could have a little piece of peach cobbler after supper.

She dug out a portion and gave it to Mae, Cater's mother, who worked as a maid for the households. She moved from house to house during the week, cleaning and washing and iron-ing, always humming some song, always keeping a look-out for us, always there, within reach.

At night I woke in the darkness of the room where Dee and I slept, and I gazed through the shadows outside the window and wondered.

It took us three weeks to scoop up and carve out the inside of the log. Then Uncle Harry said we needed to waterproof it with a solution he found in one of the out-buildings. We brushed it on like paint and let it sit for twenty-four hours "to cure," as Uncle Harry had advised.

That night we sat out on the back stoop and ate our fish with greasy hands. Sitting in a triangle in straight-back chairs at the small square table covered with newspapers, we stared out toward the water between bites.

"We gonna float down the river and find us a bed of oysters, dig 'em up and sell 'em to Leck Smalley at his store," Cater said. "Make us a dollar or two and have some good eats besides."

"That's a great idea," I said.

Dee grinned and nodded. He showed his big crooked teeth. Cousin Ruth's husband Kendall had found two old canoe paddles. We washed off the dust that had gathered through years of storage. Kendall remembered how he and Uncle Harry had built a canoe long before any of us were born. They had paddled it up into bear country and found the remains of an old Indian camp from a time when the Creeks and Choctaw lived in this wilderness. "There were some small mounds where the Indians buried warriors who died in battle," Kendall said. "There are worlds of Indian artifacts just laying on the ground up there."

"How do you know that?" I asked.

"It's told in Indian legend," he said. "I know it to be true."

"Besides, we were there," Kendall said.

I studied on that idea, which Dee said was "true as the Bible," but it still made me wonder. Cater said there were some Indians still living up in the swamp to the north. "It's desolate country up there," he said with an air of knowledge.

"I'd like to see an Indian," I said. Once, at a museum along U.S. 90 near Destin, Florida, when Daddy and Mama took us on vacation. I saw an Indian. He was a "Redskin Renegade," according to the sign. He wore artificial leather pants and a shirt with frayed tassels along the sleeves and down the outer sides of the pants. He looked sad and undernourished, on display with two lazy alligators that lay in the shade near a mud puddle. All three looked like they needed a good supper. And they smelled like rotten fish.

"I wouldn't," Dee said. His eyes were as large as Cater's. "I don't want to see a Indian or a ghost," he said.

"We might could learn something from an Indian," I said.

"Like how to build a dugout canoe?" Cater asked.

"We know how to do that," Dee said.

"Maybe he'd teach us a better way to do it," I offered.

"I doubt it," Cater said. He motioned. "We got the book, Handbook for Boys, and I'd say that's all we need."

After we finished eating and wiped off our faces, we sat on the front steps while Uncle Harry and Kendall and John rocked behind the screen. Aunt Lucille came to the front door and said, "You boys don't stay out and get eaten up by mosquitoes."

"Can we catch lightning bugs?" Dee asked.

"Go ask your mama, Cater, if she'll give y'all a fruit jar."

Dee scampered off to the back of the house to find his mother in the kitchen.

"What kind of Indians live around here?" I asked.

Aunt Lucille chuckled before she ducked back into the house.

"Aren't many Indians anymore," Uncle Harry said. "Used to be a bunch of Creeks up the river a piece."

"They were a bad bunch," John said. "They killed every last soul at Fort Mims," he added. He said it like it happened week before last.

"Fort Mims?" I asked.

"Where's Fort Mims?" Dee asked, inching a little closer to me.

"Up the river a few miles."

"Could we paddle up there?" I asked.

"I don't think I'd go that far, if I was y'all," Uncle Harry said. "It's probably fifteen, twenty miles, maybe farther."

"We went one time years ago," Kendall said.

"When you had the canoe?" I asked, remembering his tale.

He nodded. "It was beyond the remains of the old Indian village."

"Where artifacts are laying around on the ground?" I asked.

"Hush, Thomas," Dee said. "Let Daddy tell about Fort Mims."

"It's a very dark place, surrounded by thorny bushes and man-traps still set to this day. And it was nearly two-hundred years ago

that those poor people were trapped inside that fort and massa-
cred by the mad Indians. Killed five-hundred-and-some-odd, all
told," Kendall said, his voice coloring the history with mystery.
"They were old men and women and little children."

"Children?" I asked.

"Killed dozens of 'em, cut 'em open, took scalps."

Cater returned with the jar, saying, "Let's catch us some lightning bugs," but I said, "I want to hear about Fort Mims and the
massacre."

Dee rose and followed Cater. Ten feet away, Dee slapped his
hands together and announced, "I got one."

I stayed seated on the steps. "How'd the Indians kill so
many?" I inquired.

"The settlers were sleeping in the middle of the day. It was
hot, like these days, and there were thousands of mosquitoes,
big ones like out tonight, and many of the little children had
come down with the fever," Kendall explained. "Their parents
were tending to 'em."

"And some damn fool had let sand blow up against the gate
where it wouldn't close," put in John. "They didn't have the
sense or the energy to sweep the sand aside. Like Kendall said,
it was hot as blazes."

"So when the Indians came, they walked right in and started
killing, and nobody could get away. They had 'em hemmed up
in there," Kendall said authoritatively. "The Indians were mad
as hornets because white soldiers had killed a half-dozen peaceful Muskogee Creeks who'd been on a trading mission down to
Pensacola. There'd been a few skirmishes here and there, up
Burnt Corn Creek, down this way. By the time they got to Fort
Mims, they swarmed in there like a bunch of banshees and cornered men, women and children, taking 'em by surprise, and

before sundown they had killed everything white inside the log walls.

"It was the news of that tragedy, carried up to Tennessee by horseback, that angered old Andy Jackson so much he took it on himself to raise an army of volunteers and march south into Alabama and kill every Indian he could find. That's what happened up at Horseshoe Bend on the Tallapoosa River. Old Hickory they called Jackson. He slaughtered every redskin that wouldn't join up with him and give him vital information about other Indians."

"And those who joined him he later made slaves of and sent 'em packing off to Oklahoma on the Trail of Tears," Uncle Harry added. "That's how Alabama got free of renegade Indians. Or most of 'em."

"Except for those who got away and live up the river a piece," I said. I was mesmerized, taking in every word, every fact, every message, and four hours later I awakened in our dark room. I lay in the bed across from Dee, listening to his heavy snoring, gazing across the mound of his rising and falling belly, wondering whether the ghosts of all those people who were killed at Fort Mims were still wandering around in the wilderness up there just a few miles north of us.

The next morning, when we prepared to launch our dugout, I asked Dee and Cater if they wouldn't rather paddle north into the old Indian territory.

They looked at each other. They had not given it a thought. The idea all along was that we were making the dugout to go fishing, and everybody knew the best fishing was to the south. But I had been thrilled and captivated by the words of the men last night as they talked about the Fort Mims massacre, the Indian wars and General Andrew Jackson. Within moments, using the powers of persuasion I had learned from my father, a traveling salesman, I convinced both Dee and Cater that we should paddle north and take a look at the historical sites. "It's kind of like Lewis and Clark," I said.

They stared at me like I was crazy. They had not the first idea who Lewis and Clark were. And when I said, "If they hadn't taken off across the country to find the northwest passage, we wouldn't know where the Pacific Ocean was to this day," they just shook their heads.

We looked over our work one last time, savoring that moment before we discovered whether it would work or not. After slight hesitation, we slid the dugout into the dark river water. We stood back and watched anxiously as it dipped once then came up, floating. It rocked to the side, took in some water, then rolled back upright.

Cater and I steadied the boat for Dee, who climbed in awkwardly and was almost thrown over the opposite side. He grabbed the post across the middle and held himself balanced as he bent his knees and lowered himself to a sitting position. I handed over a small pail he used to dip out the water from the flat bottom.

Cater lowered himself from the pier into the front, settling on his knees, sitting back on his heels, and I did likewise in the rear, where I could paddle and guide, trying to make myself into an Indian.

Cater and I lowered our paddles into the water and started out against the current, the bow pointing northward. I maneuvered into the middle of the hundred-foot-wide water, out of the reach of the low-hanging branches of the thick brush.

Within a mile, after an hour of steady paddling, the river narrowed and the banks became more visible with large trees taking the place of the thick undergrowth. Several camp houses dotted the shoreline, set back into shadowy coves. We passed a simple plywood square with a three-by-six porch with a deer's carcass stretched between a triangle of timbers. A stench drifted to us, and Dee remarked, "Don't go no closer," and scrunched up his face.

"I wonder why..." Cater started, gazing toward the place.

I wondered who and why, and where the people were. I felt a shiver trickle down my back, then lowered my arms and paddled harder and deeper, pushing on up the river.

By mid-morning, as the sun beat down, we slowed to a crawl. We were drenched with sweat. Even Dee, who paddled occasionally, when one of us grew tired, was sweating. He knotted a handkerchief at each corner and dipped it into the water and capped it on his head to cool his scalp.

"I don't know whether we ought to keep going," Cater said, looking around at the dense woods and the bright blue sky.

But I kept pushing onward.

Dee looked from shore to shore, and in a short while pointed northwest and said, "What's that?"

The bank on the far side of a long bend was cut high and white. Above the cliff were live oaks similar to the ones at the family compound. Beyond the first growth of trees was another embankment that rose about twenty feet without trees.

"Looks interesting," I said, aiming.

"I don't know," Dee said.

"Looks kind-a spooky to me," Cater said.

"Nothing but an old Indian mound," I said. "Just like what John and Kendall were talking about last night. I bet there are worlds of Indian artifacts up there, just laying on the ground."

I guided us toward the high bank. The dugout stayed on course, exactly the way I maneuvered the paddle at the stern, the front pointing toward a sliver of white sand that shone brightly in the noonday sun.

As Cater prepared to jump into the shallows and pull us onto land, Dee said, "There ain't no Indian ghosts."

As Cater tugged the flat-bottom log toward the sand, Dee scooped up our lunch and thermos before stepping out. Cater reached to grab his meaty arm.

"I'm awright," Dee said, jerking away, avoiding assistance, stumbling and falling as if in slow motion, like Mo in The Three Stooges, reaching out with hands clawing and grasping at air.

Our lunch tumbled from his grip as his wide back splashed into the water.

"He can't swim," I uttered.

I shoved my paddle onto the bottom of the boat, stood and jumped into the river after him.

I immediately sank, the water just off the sandbar dropping to a depth over my head. I slapped out, my open palms pushing against the water, lifting myself up with the thought of grabbing Dee and pulling him to safety. But when I grabbed for him, he fought against me. His arms and shoulders were strong. They shoved against me, but I didn't give up. I swung around through the water and came up on his opposite side to surprise him and throw my arm over his shoulder. I would cup him under the chin just like the illustration in the Handbook for Boys. I would lift his head up out of the water and drag him to safety, throw his limp body onto the sandbar and straddle his body and push into his lungs and pull up on his butterflied elbows like the drawing of the two boys.

But when I came up on his left side he was so surprised, he swung around and caught me on the jaw, knocking me back into the deep water.

As I went down, falling back, Cater shouted, "Snake!"

Hearing his warning, my head ducked beneath the water. Somewhere nearby I heard them splashing. My mind held a conglomerate of ideas: Dee's drowning, Cater's being bitten by a snake, I'm...

My feet slid against an embankment of sand on the bottom of the river. The sand moved with me, giving beneath my feet, rolling, like a wave down on Dauphin Island, rolling and sliding away from me, carrying me down with it, like an undertow.

I fought. I slapped my hands against the current. I kicked. I held my lips clinched, daring not to gasp for breath, praying against any thought of drowning.

Suddenly my chest gripped hard and tight, wrenching my insides, and I was forced to open my mouth and gulp. Water poured down my throat, strangling, filling my throat and my chest, heavy, pushing against me with the weight of a heavy anvil.

Just as I thought my head was about to clear the water's edge, seeing a green light somewhere above, something big and bulky surrounded my body and jerked me free of the shifting sand.

My shoulders came up first, then my head was thrown back. I gasped and choked and coughed and spat up a knot of water lodged in my throat.

Dee threw me onto the sandbar, my shoulders hitting against the hot sand, and he lifted my arms and pushed his weight against my shoulder blades. Another blockage in my chest clamped my throat tight, like someone had their fingers wrapped around my windpipe. Dee grunted as he came down onto my back again, and again the constriction in my chest released, and water flowed from my mouth involuntarily as Dee raised my elbows and pulled them up into the air again.

"God," I exclaimed after the water rushed from my throat. "God!" I said again.

"Dee saved your life," Cater said as he dropped to his knees next to my face. From his hand hung a limp six-foot water moccasin, his black head split down the middle.

Later, while all three of us sat naked in the sunlight with our clothes drying nearby, Cater said, "I don't know how he did it. I swear I don't." His face glistened like a wet black rock. "When you came out of the boat, that snake headed for you with his head up out of the water and his tail swishing from side to side. Dee moved so fast, he caught the snake by its tail and popped him in the air like a whip or something. That ol' snake's head burst wide open. Next thing I knew, Dee had a-hold of you and was pulling you up out of the deep. You'd done slipped into that current over yonder and it was pulling you out like it had a drag-line around your ankle. But ol' Dee wouldn't let go, he had you in his hands and dragged you up onto land, you fightin' him every inch."

"But..." I started. I wanted to tell them how it was I who was going to save Dee. It was I, the Scout who was on his way toward becoming an Eagle to prove my physical and mental prowess, who planned to be the hero. Instead, I hushed. After a while, I gazed toward the high bank that held the promise of Indian mounds and artifacts. For an instant in the afternoon haze of the bright sun I thought I saw a figure standing there tall and superior, lording over this land from which he had once been chased. But when I wiped my eyes and looked again, I saw nothing there, and I never mentioned the presence to the others.

Cater had pulled our boat onto the sand. Like our clothes, it had dried. The paddles lay on each side.

We lay on the sand in the heat, resting, our bodies drying like our clothes and our boat.

Our lunch was lost, along with the thermos. We cupped river water in our hands and sipped. It soothed our throats but made our stomachs growl with hunger.

Cater stared at the high embankment. "You don't want to see some ol' Indian mounds, do you?" he asked.

"Naw," I said. "Not today."

As we climbed into the dugout, Dee said, "I can taste me some of Mama's peach cobbler."

"And a big ol' spoon of ice cream on top," Cater said.

"And a giant glass of iced tea," I said as I lowered my paddle into the water and we started moving into the middle of the river where we would catch the strong downstream current to take us home.

Next summer I took up other activities: Little League baseball and going to Scout camp, where I learned arts and crafts but was never very good at any. I did earn an Eagle badge, which made me wonder about the accomplishment. After high school I went off to college. When I returned home on holiday vacations Mama would tell me about visiting Aunt Lucille and Uncle Harry and Dee. Dee always asked about me, she said, and she would tell him about my studies, and he would grin and nod and say he would like to see me.

I was out west in graduate school one August when Mama called and reported, "Dee died last night." I felt a little catch in the back of my throat as I uttered, "Oh no." I couldn't leave to come home for the funeral. I was busy preparing some paper for my fall classes. I waited until Christmas, when I returned to our house in Tuscaloosa to sit with Mama and talk about family. One morning we rose early and I drove south to visit Aunt Lucille. Uncle Harry had died several years before and I hadn't made it home for his funeral either. Cousin Ruth and Kendall had moved away, leaving their place empty. He had gotten a high-paying job with NASA over in Mississippi. Cousin Sybil still lived next door. She came over every morning and cared for her mother. Her husband John still worked in town, leaving every morning and returning just before twilight. When he arrived, we all sat on the porch. To the slow tune of Aunt Lucille's rockingchair moving against the old boards, they talked. Sybil told how Mae and Cater had moved away years ago. They'd heard Mae died of cancer some time back. Cater, she said, had gone up north and had never been heard from since. When she said the words I hurt a little, ached inside with a longing for that afternoon when we lay naked on the sandbar and listened to the river roll by, breathing deep the clean fresh air.

In the last light, Aunt Lucille said, "I wish you could of seen Dee. He was right handsome laying on the white silk in the coffin. He looked so peaceful. Like he was asleep. You know, he found the Lord in his last days. He found the Lord and gave his soul to Jesus Christ."

For a moment I started to protest. Dee couldn't reason. He knew little or nothing about history. He had no idea how to contemplate any religion, much less Christianity.

Cousin Sybil looked toward me and nodded almost imperceptibly. Then she reached over and patted her mother on the knee. "He's in heaven, Mama."

After Aunt Lucille rocked forward and back again, a whippoorwill called from somewhere across the water. An instant later, a mockingbird answered. I hugged my arms close to my body, feeling yesterday's chillbumps as the moss began to whisper in the trees.

Jamey Conway rushed into my life like some great event—yet he was just another neighborhood kid in Cedarwood, a lower middle-class suburb of Tuscaloosa. His presence—that sad, ugly, zit-pocked, pitiful, pleading face, bulging brown eyes brimming with tears, quivering mouth drawn so tight it appeared bloodless, a high forehead extending into wisps of straw-colored hair—was a mask that dominated a season of my childhood. When I thought about him, I shivered, a reaction as involuntary as a hand jerking from flames.

Jamey Conway was two years older than I. He was bigger and meaner. He reminded me of my country cousins: wide and thick, eyes small and mean, glaring when they looked on anything, ready instantly to criticize and curse and fight, challenging.

The first time my little brother Donnie Lee met him he said Jamey was a "God-damn bully." I told Donnie Lee not to curse. At twelve, I was big on Sunday school. Brother Will, our minister, was my favorite person in the world, and he said cursing only showed you had an immature and inadequate vocabulary. After Jamey said he was going to whip the living daylights Donnie Lee and two of his buddies, Donnie Lee began carrying a Louisville slugger. If the bully came after him again, Donnie Lee swore he would take Jamey's head off.

I didn't have a run-in with Jamey until late one Saturday night when Troop 143 camped out for the weekend in the wooded area of Hackberry Park. It wasn't really woods, but we pretended. We pitched our tents, built campfires, cooked our dinner, talked about being deep in a wilderness when actually streetlights cast shadows only a hundred yards away.

We were sitting around the campfire telling stories about the last Scout Jamboree. A sound hooted from nearby trees. Like an owl, but even we knew there were no owls in a park in Tuscaloosa. Soon it sounded again, long and low, screeching, eerily.

"It's a ghost," a leader said, staring out into the thickest woods. We drew close together, scrunched tight, until our sides touched. We stared out into the darkness. Distant shadows played against the trees.

A whooping sound came, broken by laughter and guttural drunken calls from some fool who leaped from behind the trunk of a tree and swooped toward us with open arms.

Among the giddy intruders, I recognized Jamey Conway among the mocking, older boys, reckless in their beer-fogged disguise. We cowered at the sight, afraid of their banshee screeching in the night.

They danced around our fire, kicked at the coals, scattering them and setting little flames in the dry leaves, and they laughed madly until they saw Aaron Brianlevel, our Scoutmaster, stand and reach out. They skirted his reach until another of the adults corralled two near a tent.

The older boys glanced around like frightened animals, then bolted across the tarpaulin, pulling up tent pegs. They tromped over the downed tent and scampered off into the darkness. Left behind, cornered between two larger tents, was our neighbor. Standing next to Mr. Brianlevel, I uttered, "Jamey Conway."

He glared into my eyes and spat, "I'll git you! I swear I will!" Then he kicked madly at a taut line, pulling up a stake as Mr. Brianlevel grabbed his wrist and jerked him away.

Jamey kicked again. His toe hit Aaron Brianlevel's shin.

The man released his grip and bent to grab his leg.

As Jamey twisted away, he swore, "I'll git you, you little bastard!" into my face.

Then he ran into the woods. A car's tires scratched off up Hackberry Lane.

Mr. Brianlevel grilled me. At first I concealed his identity, then the Scout leader said, "You called him Jamey Conway. Does he live near you? In Cedarwood?" I looked away and nodded my head.

The next day Mr. Brianlevel and the other leaders visited Jamey's father, who was also a member of Hargrove Road Methodist church and who promised, "He'll never do that again."

After the sun went down, all through Cedarwood echoed the sounds of loud whacks of a board slapping against flesh. A man's gruff voice shouted, "You will never act a damn fool again!" Then another slam was heard, the man swinging a paddle that hit hard, relentless. In the shadows behind the Conway house a man stood in the open door of a single-car garage. Inside, another figure stood with his naked body leaning forward against a cross, his arms outstretched, hands gripping a two-by-four that crossed a vertical four-by-four. After the tenth whack, an almost imperceptible moan was heard as the naked boy's knees buckled and he crumbled against the gravel floor. "Get up!" the man commanded. He waited until the boy had pulled himself up and grasped the crossbar again, then the man hit two more licks before he turned and left the boy whimpering and shivering in the dark.

I awakened late that night. In my dreams Daddy beat me until blood ran down my legs. Mama clasped his biceps and pleaded for him to stop, but he picked up a razor strap and swung it. As it whistled through the air, I bit my tongue and awakened with a shout of "Stop!" When I opened my eyes, Mama was standing over me, her soft hands holding my shoulders, her voice saying, "Thomas, Thomas, everything's all right, son." I pulled the extra pillow to my body and hugged it, shivering.

Three days later, on my way home from school, a creature leaped from thick bushes near Bobo's creek. Recognizing the shape and frame of Jamey Conway, although he wore a Halloween mask, a black knit cap and a heavy Navy peajacket, I bolted toward the nearby sugarcane field. I had roamed here in the summertime. Beyond the heavy bushes the creek expanded to a four-foot-deep swimming hole near a shack where a family from Honduras had moved last spring. I rushed through the sugarcane, escaping Jamey Conway's fury, hovering like a coward beneath a wall of thick kudzu.

With arms wrapped around my knees, I held my breath as his footfalls stomped nearby, cursing under his breath. He drew closer and closer, and I kept my eyes shut, trying not to make a sound.

"You sorry little bastard," he cursed as he reached down and grabbed my shoulders and jerked me up.

As quickly as my feet hit the ground, they spun me away. I stumbled onto a path, losing my footing, and fell into the matted growth of thick green leaves.

With elbows and knees scraped, my insides quivering, Jamey bent down and turned me over. I stared up at him through the curtain of tears as he slammed a fist into my face.

I cried out, but he hit me again and again. In the middle of his third or fourth hit, I heard the growl of a dog. Out of the corner of my swelling eye I saw a black-and-gray splotched German shepherd bearing his teeth, snapping at Jamey's leg.

From the cane field stepped a boy larger than Jamey. Without hesitating, the stranger hit Jamey the way a football player tackles a runner. Taller and bigger, he said something in a thick accent.

After the big boy slammed against Jamey, the dog stayed with him, grabbing his pants in his jaw and jerking his head.

Without looking back, Jamey Conway scampered away as quickly as he had appeared.

The dog leaped after him, then returned when the other boy called, "Perro, stay, boy. Stay."

I found myself lying in the rich black dirt, smelling its fecund ripeness among the green plants and tasting the copper bitterness of my own blood. I was still shaking and weeping when Hector Rodriguez lifted my body and held me in his arms with my bloody, weeping face buried in his shoulder. Perro moaned and followed at his master's side as Hector carried me to my front door and Donnie Lee guided him to the backyard.

As I washed away the dirt and blood under the backyard hydrant, Mama came out in a rush. Startled, she took me in her arms and hugged me and said, "Did that boy. . ." I stood in front of her with my arms down my sides, my torn clothes soaking, my face swollen, whimpering, saying nothing.

When I saw that she was glaring at Hector, I shook my head. "No, no, no," I said.

"He helped Thomas," Donnie Lee told her.

Hector, standing like a mute giant in loose-fitting pants that fell short of his sockless brogans, looked down with big sad brown eyes. He leaned to the side and patted the dog's head.

"I'm sorry," Mama muttered.

Not uttering a word, Hector turned and walked away, the dog following.

I called after him. Donnie Lee ran to catch him and thank him for his help.

Mama fussed over me and instructed Donnie Lee to go inside and fetch iodine. Painting my cuts and scraps, Mama whined that she was sorry for the way she attacked Hector, but said he was "such a big, strange-looking boy." Then she stopped suddenly and looked into my eyes. "Who did this?" she asked.

I said nothing.

"Was it that Conway boy?" she started. "It was, wasn't. . ."

She did not finish before she stomped off across the back-yard, cutting across two neighbors' yards, crossing a street. In the distance I heard her rapping on the door of the Conway house. Then I heard her scream, "Your son is a menace!"

In the darkness after supper I heard the whacks again. They came, it seemed, a minute apart. A heavy, hard sound. Then silence. It seemed such a long time between strikes. I lay in my bed with my own hurt, the pain of his violence wrapping around me like a thick scratchy blanket. Each time the thick wooden slat jolted against Jamey Conway's blistered, battered bottom, my own wounds jerked with intense pain. When I closed my eyes, the pain intensified, coursing through my veins and nerves, causing me to wince, then hold my breath while wondering if the last was truly the last. Then another came.

I fell asleep in the agony of the distant punishment. The incessant sound, unbearably slow and eternal, echoed into the night.

The next afternoon I walked home across the broad field of the Abernathy farm where thick green grass grew between expanses of neat white-painted fences. With me was my newest friend, Hector Rodriguez, and his black-muzzled dog Perro, who waited for his owner at the edge of the schoolyard. Before yesterday I had known Hector only as a boy from Honduras who was two years older and two feet taller, the only boy in our class with a tattoo, a blue-and-red scorpion on his left ankle. He was the best marble-shooter in the seventh grade. He had bigger hands, longer fingers. He owned three cat-eyes, a midnight-black with a milky streak and a half-dozen spotted Jacks. A mop of coal-black hair covered Hector's head and his skin was the shade of chocolate milk. Before yesterday, I had been afraid of Hector Rodriguez. He was different, odd-looking in his ragged clothes, and he talked funny. I had been guilty of joining other students who laughed at him behind his back. But when he circled my shoulders with his thick-muscled arm and said, "Don't worry about this boy, Jamey. If he comes close to you, I will take care of him," I felt secure. His accent was thick and his dark eyes sparkled as he said, "If I catch him, he will hurt. If Perro catch him, he will tear him to pieces." He smiled, showing big yellow teeth. "I haven't had a good fight since we left Honduras." From the bulging pocket of the same baggy pants he had been wearing yesterday, he withdrew a bone-handle switchblade six-inches long. He snapped the release and the blade, long and slender and shining like polished silver, clicked out in a snap. He slid his thumb over the blade and smiled with a mean grin and said, "I could slit him from his gonads to his goozle," and I felt a shiver crawl down my sides. Perro growled, like an echo.

In the weeks ahead, Hector, who had made F's in most subjects until I started sliding my paper to the corner of my desk and turning it so he could read my words or my numbers, began to appreciate my efforts to enlighten his education and raise his grades. "My mother smile when I bring her my report card with C's and D's. She was afraid I would never make it in the schools here." Hector smiled and nodded. He squeezed my shoulder and said, "She did not know I would have such a good teacher."

For several weeks Jamey Conway disappeared from school and the neighborhood. Donnie Lee said he heard Jamey was taken to the hospital. Mama, who was assistant administrator at the hospital, reported that he had not been admitted. Then Donnie Lee overheard gossip at Grady's Store that Jamey had been carried to a private clinic in Birmingham. All we knew was that he was absent from our world.

Late in the day we sat in the field of clover, smelling its fresh flavor mixed with the ripe odor of cow manure. When Jamey Conway didn't show, we relaxed and wandered over to the four-room square-frame house where Hector and his mother and three little sisters lived. On the town side of Bobo's creek, it was owned by real estate magnate, Leland Abernathy, who rented it, until Hector's family moved in, to Negroes who worked on his farm. Hector said his mother and Mr. Abernathy had "an arrangement." We sat on the edge of the front porch. Perro lay in the shade, watching. Mrs. Rodriguez fix a pitcher of grape Kool-Aid. Carla eight; Tina six, and Frida four let the blue liquid run down their chins, streaking and spotting their meager clothes, and they giggled and giggled, until little Frida wet her pants. "You were clean," Mrs. Rodriguez said in an accent thicker than her son's. "I'll get them, Mama," Hector said, grabbing Frida up from the dirt, whisking off her dirty pants and carrying her to the creek under his arm, where she kicked and screamed. Behind them, Perro barked and jumped joyfully. Hector stepped into the water, dousing the little girl, and she jiggled with laughter. The other two joined them, splashing and laughing. From the porch, Mrs. Rodriguez handed down three towels. "Would you take, please, Thomas?" I took the towels to Hector, who began drying the three little girls and handing them to me. I took each around the waist, their bare bottoms dripping, and carried them to their mother. Finished, Hector clasped me on the back. "What about a bath, amigo?" he asked. I shook my head. "I better be going," I said, and started for the bridge.

When I got home, Donnie Lee asked in a rushed voice if I'd heard the latest news. "Jamey Conway was sitting on his front steps this afternoon glaring at everybody who walked by."

"I didn't see him," I said.

'You're the only one," Donnie Lee said.

The next afternoon Hector and I walked together. Donnie Lee stayed at school to play ball with other third-graders.

When we got to the little house next to the creek a long brown Lincoln Continental sat on the sandy circle in front of the porch. Hector led the way around the big car, looking inside its tinted windows, and I followed, looking in at a pile of magazines on the backseat and a nickel-plated pistol on the splendid leather seat behind the shiny wood-grained veneer of the dashboard with its speedometer, radio, heater-air-conditioner and glove compartment.

"Guess Mama left the girls with Thelma," Hector whispered. Thelma was a neighbor down the dirt road, where Mrs. Rodriguez worked part-time making drapes for rich women in Thelma's basement. "Stay," Hector commanded Perro, who dropped to his hindquarters. He motioned to me. "Come on," he said, and I followed around the corner of the house and up an embankment to a thicket of pine saplings, where he crouched in the darkness and gazed down across the ravine toward the house.

I too stared at the open window. In the shadows was the figure of a woman. Heavy-hipped with the same honey-brown skin as Hector, her large naked breasts were as tan as her swaying belly and the thick trunk-like thighs that emerged from white underpants. I gasped as I gazed and gasped again as she hooked her thumbs over the elastic top of the underwear and pushed down and stepped out of them one foot at a time, revealing a thick patch of black hair between her legs.

Hearing the subtle rustle of dry pine straw, I looked over at Hector, whose eyes were intent on the scene. I blinked and caught my breath. A part of me wanted to turn and run. Another wanted to join in the animal-like sexual heat of the moment. But this was Hector's mother; she was not supposed to be sexy. Hector had pulled his penis free of his pants.

I stood as still as a statue, my heart beating like a parade drum, my throat going dry. I wanted to run but I couldn't make my feet step away from the spot.

I stared through the window, watching Mrs. Rodriguez moving slowly in the shadows, like she was dancing a one-woman waltz. From behind the curtains stepped a man. He too was naked. His arms opened. He wrapped them around her body and pulled her away from the window.

I inched away, trying to crawl quietly out of the thicket.

"Thomas, mi amigo," Hector said.

"I'll see you tomorrow," I whispered, turning and trying to climb down the embankment without a sound. On several loose rocks I lost my footing and started slipping. I worked my feet fast to keep from sliding. I grabbed a pine sapling that bent with my weight. From the window I heard someone say, "What's that. . ." But I didn't stop. I kept moving down the hillside, tumbling once, then regaining balance and running past Perro toward the bridge beyond the brown Lincoln.

By the time I got home I was out of breath. I had moved full speed through the neighborhood, not bothering to stop when someone shouted my name, thinking I had to get inside my room and close the door. When I got there I fell onto the bed.

Donnie Lee came in and asked me something and I mumbled a reply. Mama came in later and asked how my day went. All through supper I wanted to say something to somebody. I wanted to tell them what I had seen and the crazy mixed-up feelings that were soaring through my brain. But I said nothing.

After doing my homework, I lay in the silent darkness. It was darker than ever. When shadows floated from the window across the ceiling, I pictured images of evil. The sight of Mrs. Rodriguez swirled through my head: her drooping large breasts, her brown belly, the triangle of black at the top of her legs, her midnight-black hair falling down over her shoulders. Protestant confusion overwhelmed me with guilt, and when I shut my eyes the images did not go away. And I could not drive the memory of Hector from my mind.

On the next morning in the bright sunshine of the school playground, Hector walked toward me with his rolling gait, grinning. I wanted to turn away and run back home. Who would I rather face? Him? Or Jamey Conway?

"Mi amigo," Hector said in his pleasant accent.

I said nothing but didn't turn away. When he clasped me across the back I walked with him. I shrugged my shoulders and kept up with him step-for-step. He didn't say a word about what we had seen. At afternoon recess he asked if I'd heard any news about Jamey. I shrugged. Two hours later, after the last bell, we were met by Perro and started toward the Abernathy farm where a figure lurked in the shadows of four oak trees. "Is that him?" Hector asked.

I squinted but could not make out the details of the dark figure standing next to the largest tree. By the way he slouched to one side with his head cocked, I was sure it was Jamey. "Will you go with me?" I whispered to Hector.

"Of course, mi amigo," he said, and he slapped me across the shoulder in his jovial way. His eyes were just as brightly dark as always.

We moved out, Perro nearby. We picked up the pace while my heart beat hard and my mind wondered if I could run all the way across the pasture, over the hill, and down through the first woods to Hector's mother's house. Maybe, if Mr. Abernathy was there with his pistol. . .

When we got to the place near the trees, we found no one. Perro sniffed at the roots but made no sound. Perhaps I had imagined the sight, but Hector had also seen him. I said nothing, praying.

I sat on the largest root and caught my breath, resting in the shade. I looked out across the pasture toward the cows grazing in the distance. I saw no one. Perro came to me. I rubbed his black nose and he wagged his tail.

When Hector came back around, I looked up at him. Sweat covered his face but his breath was easy. He put his hand on my shoulder. "We'll walk with you all the way home," he volunteered.

We walked. Before we crossed the creek I slowed to see if the big brown Lincoln was at the house again. It wasn't. The three little girls played on the porch and waved to their brother. He called that he would return soon.

The rest of the way was calm. If Jamey Conway had wanted to scare me, he succeeded. At my house I thanked Hector and rushed inside. No one else was home. I lay on my bed and closed my eyes. I thought what a great friend Hector was. I didn't even have to ask him to walk home with me. He just came.

I dozed. I awakened to a noise. I lay still. At first I imagined Jamey Conway breaking into the house and entering my room with an ax. I listened.

From the central hall I heard, "Thomas?" and took a deep breath and rose and went to the door. When I saw Mama's outline, I wanted to reach out and pull her into my arms. I didn't.

I followed her into her and Daddy's bedroom, where she kicked off shoes and began pulling off stockings. Mama was always bigger than she seemed; a slight woman with bones like a bird's. Although delicately made, she gave me a sense of strength, energy and knowledge: knowing far more than she would ever say. When she had changed to slacks and a pullover shirt, she looked at me and said, "What's wrong?" And when I said, "Nothing," her high forehead wrinkled.

In the kitchen, while she made dinner, I put plates onto the table and said, "I thought Jamey Conway was waiting on me in the pasture at Abernathy's farm."

"You want me to pick you up after school?"

"No, ma'am," I said.

Most afternoons I liked walking home after school. It was fun to sit in the high grass at Abernathy's farm and cross the creek at Hector's mother's house and steal a stalk of sugarcane from

Bobo's patch and strip it down and take it into the thick dark kudzu caverns and sit in my own private lair and chew the sinewy fibers and taste the sweetness seep down my throat.

"Want me to arrange for you to ride with one of the other mothers?"

"I don't think so," I said.

"You're not afraid?"

"No, ma'am," I lied.

She put her hand behind my head, cradling me gently. "You're a big boy," she said, and I wished I felt like a big boy.

After supper, I ambled out the back door. I sat on the steps and looked out between the houses of our neighborhood in the direction of the Conway house. Lights shone there. Now and then a figure walked across a window. But I could not tell if it was Jamey.

That evening I lay awake. Images of his fists slamming against my face flashed through my memory. Then I saw Hector's mother naked in her house. On the bed in the shadows was the figure of Jamey Conway, pale and thick and surly, his mouth twisting into a snarl, laughing dryly, his large brown penis pointing toward her as she moved silently toward him.

When I awakened in the middle of the night, I was shivering. In her nightgown, Mama lowered herself onto my bed and wrapped her arms around my body and held me securely. I felt the warmth of her soft breast against my cheek. "You were dreaming, Thomas. A nightmare." She rocked me from side to side. "Are you all right, son?" she asked.

"Yes, ma'am," I said.

"You sure?"

I nodded.

For three afternoons, Hector and I walked guardedly to the bottom of Abernathy farm. Perro stood next to us, gazing out across the pasture, tail alert.

The next day at recess I saw Jamey Conway. He was standing near the playground. He was staring directly at me, and I felt the shiver of a nightmare climb my backbone.

When the sunshine struck him full in the face, I no longer saw a boy. He had aged years in the last few weeks. His eyes had broadened. They had sunk deeper into his face. His cheekbones were thicker, stronger, covered with pinkish skin dotted by zits, some bleeding where he had scratched. His shoulders still sagged. He slouched to the left and cocked his head in the same direction. His mouth was thin and colorless.

"He's challenging us," Hector said.

"Well?" I asked nervously. "What're we going to do?"

Hector slapped his steady hand onto my back. "Let's go."

I held back, but Hector stepped forward. Without turning, he said, "Come on."

"But school's still in," I said.

"Don't matter," Hector said. He strode straight ahead toward Jamey Conway. I had to skip a few steps to catch up.

"There's still an hour left," I said.

"They won't miss us," Hector said.

I had never skipped school. I'd played sick a time or two. But I had never played hooky, although it'd crossed my mind a number of times. I turned and looked back at the other kids playing, standing around, some of them watching us.

I followed Hector, knowing I was doing wrong and feeling guilty with every step. Nevertheless, I did not turn around.

Somewhere ahead of us, Jamey Conway skittered about through the dusky shadows and the steamy curls of heat that rose from the baked heaps of cow dung. At the hammock of trees, where black and white spotted dairy cows lazed in the shade, he escaped our sight, dancing ahead like a stick-figure over the next fence and across the broad pasture where beef cattle grazed.

Halfway across, watching him disappear up the pathway into the woods this side of Hector's house, we stopped. Hector turned, squinting into the sun. "What you reckon that crazy sonofabitch is up to?" he asked. I shrugged. With another thought, Hector did a quick about-face and began trudging his long-strided gait. I kicked up my pace, hearing him mumble, "If that crazy sonofabitch's heading for our house, I'll. . ." I stumbled, almost fell. I didn't dare tell him my dream. He didn't slow as we got within sight of the creek.

Hector was huffing as he stopped on the bald ridge and watched Jamey on the far side of the bridge disappear down into the jungle-like growth of the sugarcane field and the kudzu-draped ravine beyond. "He's going home," I said between deep breaths as I pulled up along-side my friend.

"He's just taunting us, wanting to suck us into his trap," Hector said.

"He doesn't need a trap," I said.

"To catch both of us he does," Hector said.

"We'll wait him out," I said.

"With patience and understanding," he said.

"Cunning," I said. "I don't think he has cunning."

Hector looked into my face. He was squinting again. Otherwise, I could not read his expression, although he looked like an Indian far older than his years.

To the right, beyond the ridge, the long brown Lincoln sat on the sandy yard. I thought about the gun on the front seat. A smile flashed across Hector's face. "You want to. . ." He gestured toward the pine thicket on the hillside above the house. "I better be going on home," I said, then glanced with more than a little apprehension toward the cane field and the dark green wall of kudzu. "I'll go with you," he said, then glanced toward the quiet little house again before leading the way.

We didn't see Jamey Conway for a week. We felt his presence every time we walked through the kudzu-shadowed curtain from the sugarcane field to Hargrove Road and beyond. We talked about him in low-sounding whispers, like he could hear if we talked out loud. But we did not see him. On the morning after we had last seen Jamey, Hector met me on the playground before school. Worry creased his face. "Did you notice yesterday afternoon, Perro wasn't with us? He wasn't at home either. I haven't seen him. Not a sign."

Across Abernathy's farm every afternoon we looked anxiously for the dog and for Jamey Conway. We saw only cows and piles of their dung. Donnie Lee said he'd heard Jamey had been sent to live with kinfolks in Mobile. But late the next afternoon we heard a basketball bouncing in the Conway backyard, and Donnie Lee said someone was shooting hoops. Listening to the faraway, ghostly bounce of the ball after twilight, bouncing in the light of the moon and the stars, I sat on our back steps and wondered and felt fear creep through my body, down to my bones.

The next day in a crowded hallway at school, I felt and heard heavy breathing behind me. I wheeled around. Jamey Conway stood three feet away between two girls. He grinned. The zits were worse than ever. His eyes stared into mine, burning like twin fires. He said nothing. I gasped and turned away, moving with the crowd, feeling his presence behind me.

Every time I went into the hall I looked both ways. Among the crowd of students, I didn't see him. I told Hector what had happened. He smiled and nodded and said, "He knows he's got your goat. He's playing games."

"Well," I said, "he's doing what he wants to do: scaring the shit out of me."

"Don't be scared," Hector said. "I'll be right behind you."

Again that afternoon, Jamey appeared to dance ahead of us, moving from tree to tree, bush to bush, slithering across the hot pasture, finally disappearing again over the bridge and into the cane field.

At the bridge, Hector said, "Let's set a trap for him. I'll run on ahead, cut through the back side of Bobo's place, around behind the church, on the other side of the kudzu. You stay on the path. Act like you don't care where he is or what he's up to."

"How can I do that?" I asked incredulously.

"Play act. Whistle up a tune, if you can."

I chuckled nervously and shook my head.

"Go on," he said. "Make it look good. I promise, I'll be close by. If he tries something, I'll be on him like stink on shit."

I smiled, but I felt less and less confident as I watched his long-stride lope, moving through the cane patch and disappearing into the thick woods. I took a deep breath, felt a knot of fear as hard as rock swell in my breast, and I started down the well-worn path. I tried to whistle a tune but couldn't get it started. Every time I'd pucker and blow, nothing would come out but air.

I moved into the thick dark kudzu wall between the dense rows of cane and the red-clay embankment that led to the

Cedarwood Methodist Church where every Tuesday evening
Boy Scout troop 143 met. I stepped gingerly through the shadowy world.

In the darkness covered by the broad-leaf kudzu that climbed
with an unforgiving hunger over pine and oak and hickory, I
heard scratchy sounds to the north. I prayed it was Hector, making his way ahead. Then I heard another noise south toward
Hargrove Road. I stopped. I sucked in a deep heavy breath of
damp air. It tasted like impending rain. Suddenly, for some reason, I prayed for rain, but I heard no thunder, and I knew the
darkness was the jungle-like growth blocking sunlight.

I stepped forward. My forehead hit a vine. It swung out, away
from me, then back. I ducked.

Suddenly the entire world went silent.

Overhead, a twig snapped.

My heart raced.

Twenty feet ahead, on the trunk of a thick tree, my eyes
focused on a makeshift sign with scrawling letters in white paint:
GIV UP, ASS HOL!

I glanced through the shadows. I saw nothing but the quick
frantic movement of birds in the trees beyond the sign. In the
distance a truck changed gears as it ground its way up the hill
past Abernathy farm, then changed again as it leveled off and
headed around the curve in front of the church. Exasperated,
I rushed to the sign and ripped it from the tree. Holding it
against my chest, like a shield, I picked up speed and, in less
than a minute, stepped through the last layer of kudzu like it
was a gate.

The sun sliced downward from a western slant, thick with
humidity, as I marched past the high bank of red clay and the
white-washed concrete-block church. At Grady's Store, with its

own white block walls and windows covered with signs announc-
ing this week's specials, I felt enormously strengthened, even
when I searched the perimeters and could not find Hector. As I
walked past the store on the opposite side of the double-lane
asphalt, a figure sitting on steps leading up to an old abandoned
house stated, "He's long gone."

I halted. I gasped. My heart skipped. Staring into his face, my
own suddenly covered with a layer of hot sweat, I said, "You
sonofabitch, you scared me so bad my heart dropped through my
ass."

Hector laughed. "I'd like to see that."

I sat on the step beneath him, breathed deep, and handed the
sign up to him. He stared at it, his brown brows pinching. "Just
wants to scare you," he said, handing it back.

"And he can't spell," I said.

"Oh," Hector said, and glanced back toward the sign in my
hand.

I regarded him again and realized he had no idea what I was
talking about.

That night, with the sign resting on my desk, I lay awake and
tried to comprehend my universe: the area between this house in
a quiet suburb, its narrow winding streets surrounded by wood-
lands, a stretch of Hargrove Road, our major thoroughfare, the
layer of thick kudzu-covered jungle, the sugarcane field, the
creek, Hector's house, and the long pasture that sloped down to
the broad schoolyard. And the two people I knew best between
here and there, my best friend and my enemy, were both illiterate.

At least, when I showed the sign to my little brother, Donnie
Lee grinned and said, "The fool doesn't know how to spell."

On Friday night, after Mama and Daddy fixed us hot dogs,
Cokes and potato chips, then left for a steak supper at the Elk's

Club, Donnie Lee and I, armed with hammer and nails, sneaked out the back, across our neighbors' yards, and up the Conway driveway to the garage. Beneath the light of a near-full-moon we gazed upon the wooden cross where Jamey had been punished. "Damn," Donnie Lee whispered. Then we spotted the hefty wooden slat, four-inches wide and an inch thick. The wide end was streaked with dark dried blood. Seeing it, Donnie Lee frowned. I did too, and shook my head. We heard a movement in the yard. We froze. The back door of the house opened. Someone stepped out. We heard a voice from inside but could not make out the words. Footsteps crushed against thick grass, moving across the yard toward the garage. We held our breaths. I knew my brother could hear the heavy pounding of my heart. Then, on the opposite side of the garage wall, came a spewing sound. From the back door, a woman called, "I told you not to pee in the yard," and the man near us finished, zipped his pants, and said, "It's my yard, I'll piss in it if I want." A moment later the door slammed shut. Donnie Lee laughed shortly. "Let's put the sign up and get out of here." We didn't use the hammer and nails. We leaned the sign against the middle of the wooden cross where it could not be missed, only Donnie Lee added two letters in his crayons, making it read: GIVe UP, ASS HOLe!

Late the next Monday morning in the school hallway I felt him before I saw him. I knew he was behind me. I waited until the hall filled with students. I stopped in mid-stride, wheeled, and grabbed him around the neck and jerked him to the floor before he knew what was happening. I twisted his right arm behind his back and pushed it up with all my strength. He was struggling, kicking, and girls were squealing, and other boys were backed against the wall of lockers, staring at us in amazement.

When the teachers, Miss Judy Darby and Hiram Longshore, bent over us, she grabbing me by my collar and Longshore taking over my hold on Jamey's right arm, I let out a long sigh. As soon as we were on our feet, Jamey lunged from the teacher's grip, swung at me, his fist catching me in the upper ribcage, bending me double, knocking the breath from my body. As I crumbled forward, holding my side, Jamey bolted through the crowd. Miss Darby and Mr. Longshore squatted next to me as I writhed on the tile floor. When I opened my eyes I was staring directly into the white V-shaped front of Miss Darby's panties. Quickly, I rolled over onto my stomach. I moaned, holding to my side, and Mr. Longshore called two eighth graders to help lift me.

After the school nurse checked my cut and several bruises, declaring me okay, at afternoon recess I told Hector I was heading out for a show-down with Jamey Conway while I had the courage built up. I was tired of playing games. If he hadn't run away from school, I would have whipped him, or vice versa. "He might be older and bigger than me," I said. "But I know now I have a chance if I face him. I won't, if I don't."

He started to walk with me, but I stopped. "You can't go," I told him.

"I have to," Hector insisted.

"No," I said. "It's like I told you, Hector. I've got to do this. Just me. If I don't, he'll still be lurking behind every bush, every tree, around every corner, every time I walk down a hallway at school, walk through the pasture or on the streets of Cedarwood."

Reluctantly, Hector stayed behind. I didn't go the usual route. I cut over onto Hargrove Road. Carrying my books, I thumbed. The fourth car that passed was Mr. Summerford, who also lived in Cedarwood. "You been in a fight, Thomas?" he asked after I climbed into the front seat next to him.

"Yes, sir," I said.

"With that Conway boy?"

"How'd you know?"

"He's a mean one. I suspect all boys your age will get into a fight with him sooner or later."

He let me out in front of our house and wished me luck.

I pitched my books onto the front stoop and headed directly toward the Conway house. As I rounded the front corner in the driveway, Jamey's voice said, "What do you think you're doing?"

"I'm coming after you, Jamey Conway, so come on out and let's have at it."

"Hey," Jamey said, stepping from behind a bush. He held his hands out and up. "There's no reason for us to fight." Behind his hands, with fingers spread wide, he was grinning wickedly.

I balled my fists, not trusting him.

"We've already fought," he said. "You got the best of me. And I saw you looking up ol' Miss Darby's dress. Got a good look at her snatch, didn't you?"

I didn't answer. I seethed, thinking about his knowing what I had seen, knowing my secret, infuriating me even more.

"Hey, man, there's no reason for me and you to be against one another. You and your little brother got more guts than anybody I know. I admire guts."

"What about Donnie Lee?"

"He carried that baseball bat to hit me with." He chuckled. "Think I didn't know about that?"

"Well. . ."

"He'd hit me too, if he'd seen me."

I agreed.

"And then y'all slipped over here at night with that sign that stupid Honduran hodo hung in the trees."

"You did that," I accused.

He shook his head. "Hector Honduras. He thinks he's a bad ass. He's so big and so stupid. Think I don't know how to spell asshole?"

I frowned, thinking.

"He ask you for a dollar to fuck his old lady?"

"No," I said, but the vision of Hector on the hillside looking down through the window at his mother flashed through my memory.

"You're lying, Thomas Reed," he said. "That's something I didn't think you'd do, is lie. You a Boy Scout, and everything."

"I'm not lying."

"You know Hector Honduras is evil, don't you? He's a regular devil in disguise, got a foot-long dong on him, and he's screwing his own old lady. I mean, if that ain't weird, I don't know what is. You know all about him, don't you?"

I didn't answer.

"I thought so," he said. "He's the one who's been scaring you all this time, making you think it was me."

"But it was. . ."

Grinning, he said, "It was me the first time. Hector and I planned it that way, where he'd show up and be the big hero. Then he'd get on your good side, you'd help him with his homework, and maybe you'd even spring for a few bucks to be with his old lady. He take you up on the hill to look at her?"

He made me think. He forced thoughts into my head I would never have thought. Hector was my friend. Yet. . .

"Come on in here and let me show you something," he said, the smile holding.

I followed him into the cavern-like darkness of the single-car garage. Just as my foot touched the bottom extension of the four-by-four, he said, "Careful, don't trip over the crucifix," then he laughed, loud and high-pitched.

I glared through the darkness, trying to see him, but the sunbeams through the small window on the western wall, where we had heard his father peeing, shone so brightly in one spot that I could not see beyond, like a solid column.

After his laughter died, he said, "Get it? The cross, the crucifix, where my father crucified his only forgotten son?"

I shivered with the thought, but said nothing. When I stepped past the bright beams my eyes adjusted and focused on a tortured face and a stiff body hanging from the rafters. "My God," I uttered, drawing a deep breath. I was staring directly into the cold face and frizzy fur of Perro, Hector's dog. It was stretched out on a rack. "Did you. . ." I started.

Jamey held a bone-handled dagger-like knife in his right palm. It was the same straight-blade weapon that Hector had displayed weeks ago.

At the back wall of the garage Jamey opened a freezer. A light shone from within. He extracted something I didn't recognize until he held it up and waved it in the air. It was easily recognizable, even in the shadows: the frozen skinned carcass of an animal.

I pivoted and ran from the garage. I tripped over the end of the four-by-four, fell onto the gravel outside, and my stomach exploded. I heaved and heaved while Jamey laughed wildly from the bowels of the garage. I went home and was sick again. When Mama came home she said I looked awful. I told her I came home early from school, sick, and she believed me.

The next morning I confessed that I'd been in a fight with Jamey Conway. She said she knew. I had looked so ill the night before she did not have the heart to punish me. She said it was good that I told the truth. But I never told her the whole truth. I told her I needed a ride from school in the afternoon. She arranged rides with several mothers when she could not pick us up. Even if I had to wait thirty minutes or longer, it was all right. Several times Hector asked me to walk with him, but I declined. He acted like it hurt his feelings but I told him I just couldn't do it. I never told him about Perro, and I wondered if he knew, or would ever know. As for me, I thought about a lot of things.

She looked dirty. I thought she needed a bath. Seeing her seated on the back of Jake Sims's motorcycle, having graduated from a Cushman scooter to a full-fledged Harley-Davidson, I wanted to put her in a hot bath and scrub her bony body. I wanted to make her shine.

When Jake hollered above the growl, "Hey, Thomas, this is Angie," she grinned widely. She had a round, white, country face, a perky nose sprinkled lightly with freckles, tiny ears, and sunken cheeks, and the gap in her upper teeth made her resemble a cartoon chipmunk. Her breasts, no larger than half-grown lemons, poked straight out, miniature nipples stretching against the cotton tee shirt.

"Hey," she said, and stuck out her right hand, showing dirt under her nails. As soon I took it, I dropped her fingers that were stained brown and smelled of stale tobacco.

Later, Jake said, "What the hell's wrong with you, man? You got that little girl spooked, acting like you're some kind of stuck-up, better than me and her and everybody else. You acting like that, while I've been talking us up to her."

"That wasn't my intention. I just. . . Hell, Jake, she's got dirt under her fingernails and her fingers are stained tobacco brown."

"Holy shit, Mr. Clean! Don't look at her fingers. Stare into her big brown eyes and tell her how pretty they are, forget the fucking nails. Besides, her old man makes her pick corn and tomatoes, butterbeans and squash, and help her mama clean the house before she can go out. She's got a mean-ass brother who probably beats shit out of her now and then, just for the hell of it. Under the circumstances, you'd smoke too."

"She can wash before she goes out."

"You sure as hell are picky, all of a sudden."

"I swear, Jake, where'd you find her?"

"At my Granddaddy's church," he said.

Like mine, Jake's maternal grandparents were primitive Baptists. His went to a church south of Tuscaloosa, mine north. Both families were poor farm people worshiping in a simple, straight-forward, fundamentalist fashion. They were strict with their children, even after they'd grown up. They made 'em work hard for whatever they got. After that, they sort of looked past them, like the work cleansed them of any other sin. My great aunt and uncle and all of my cousins were primitive Baptists. And most of my cousins were mean as angered rattlers, true believers in the Ku Klux Klan, and drank moonshine out of fruit jars. But every second Sunday they sat in the churchhouse and praised the Lord loud and clear.

I was a Presbyterian. Even after Daddy quit going because Brother Will Armstrong invited black professors from Stillman College to worship in our church, Mama and I kept going every Sunday. I thought Brother Will was about the best person and the most courageous I'd ever known in my young life. Just talking to Brother Will was like drinking from a fountain where the water gave you an inner strength.

"She's more'n a year older'n us," Jake said. We were both sixteen, soon to be seventeen. I had had my driver's license six months. "I think, if we play our cards right, we'll be getting us a little before summer's over. I've already felt her up pretty good." Jake stuck his finger to my face. I sniffed but didn't smell anything but stale smoke.

The promise of actually "getting a little" ran through my head with more than a small thrill. I cleaned her up in my mind. She became as lovely as a movie star, like a country version of Debbie Reynolds or Jane Powell, my favorites. And when Jake called in the middle of the week, he announced, "I'm working closer and closer. By next week, I'll hit a home run." Never much of a baseball player, I dismissed the analogy and began to picture erotic scenes from a harem movie I had seen last winter: half-clad girls lounging around a steamy pool, waiting for the sultan's call.

Late on Tuesday morning, Jake called and asked if I could meet him at his old uncle's house down by the railroad tracks near the AG&S depot. I said I would, then began figuring ways of transportation. Daddy was out of town. Mama had driven her car to work. I emptied my piggy bank of fourteen dollars and eighty-three cents, figuring I might need a little extra change, especially if we took Angie anywhere. I didn't know where we'd actually take her. I just thought you usually took girls somewhere after, if not before.

I walked up to Grady's Store on Hargrove Road where I waited in the bright sunshine for the city bus that was running ten minutes behind schedule. I got on and sat directly behind the driver where I could watch every turn as we moved slowly toward town. I directed him to stop a block short of the depot, then I walked with a head full of crazy dreams to the old ramshackle Victorian house with its wide porch and high gabled roof and peeling paint. Jake's old uncle, Morris Sims, sat in the creaky swing on the porch watching me climb the steps. His eyes were small and beady and watery bloodshot. When I reached the top, sweating and nearly out of breath, Morris, grinning with a mouth full of yellow crooked teeth, said, "Jake's upstairs screwing. He said for us to wait our turn down here," and he grinned his snaggle-tooth grin again. Uncle Morris and his flat nasal words made me feel quickly queasy, made me want to turn and run, made me picture once again the girl's dirty nails and stained fingers. I glared into the grizzly old face of Morris, who was only the second person I'd ever seen drink hard whiskey before lunchtime. The first had been my next door neighbor, Ralph Williams, whom I'd caught swilling Canadian Club and Coca-Cola on the Saturday morning of my thirteenth birthday, a monumental occasion in my life.

I sat in a rocking chair opposite Morris and stared into his unshaven face framed in shaggy gray hair. Morris walked with a limp, the result of his hip catching shrapnel on his third day of combat on the Pacific island of Guadalcanal in World War Two. He called it his "million-dollar wound." Morris had not worked a day since, returning home to this house, outliving his elderly mother and father, and now residing here alone with an occasional female friend from one of the local taverns or a drop-in overnight visit from his favorite nephew. When Jake and I grew desperate for a beer, we'd visit Morris, who always kept a six-pack or two of Country Club malt liquor and a partial bottle of Four Roses blended whiskey in his refrigerator. He never seemed to run out.

"Little ol' gal wanted a sip of wine to steady her nerves," Morris said. "I had a little Thunderbird ol' Maggie left last week." Maggie was a high-yeller who cleaned house for him on the days after his monthly check came in. By the middle of each month she tended to drift off toward another source of income. I would have never known she was "high-yeller," if Jake hadn't told me; I thought she was Chickasaw or Choctaw or perhaps gypsy, but Jake said, "Her lineage goes straight back to a plantation house in Greene County," which told me everything and nothing.

"Little ol' gal kinda on the scrawny side," Morris judged as he rocked, glaring out into nowhere, swinging easily and noisily.

I didn't say anything.

From the shady side of the screendoor, Jake said, "I guess you're used to screwing Marilyn Monroe."

I squinted and saw that Jake was wearing only his jockey shorts. His sudden appearance, reminding me of the promise that waited somewhere in the darkness of the old house, sent a wave of nervousness through me. New sweat popped onto my brow.

As he said, "Come on in, Thomas," I tried to keep my knees from knocking, frightened in my eagerness, blinded by the carnal possibilities. I stepped to the door.

Morris complained, "When do I get my turn?"

Jake said, "You come in too, Morris, I've got to talk with you," and motioned me up the stairs.

As I climbed, the screendoor slammed shut and Morris said too loud, "What's there to talk about?"

"Come back here with me," Jake directed him toward the rear kitchen.

Each step became more difficult. Each time my foot put down on the worn pine floor it felt as though it would slide from under me. My entire body grew heavier and heavier, slower, as though a magnet of conscience was holding me back, asking if this was right, knowing that I was about to commit a terrible sin and feeling weighted down by all of those years of Baptist and Presbyterian teachings, the words of Granddaddy's many

preachers and Brother Will, knowing that God Himself was looking down on me with disbelief and dishonor, for I was a child of
God, washed in the blood of the lamb. I honored my father and
my mother, my grandfathers and grandmothers, all of my ances-
tors.

Jake had already told me he'd met the girl at church, had spoken
to her about his own strong religious beliefs, and had encouraged
her to open herself to both of us. There was no telling what Jake
had told her. Jake and I were the same age, but sometimes I
thought he was at least three years older. While I was frightened of
such verbal fortitude, Jake knew no bounds for boldness.

The heavy hand of a questioning conscience held to my shoulder, yet I pushed onward, stepping into the second-floor hallway
where ancient portraits of Jake's great-grandparents looked stern-
ly down on me as I squeezed open the ancient door into the bedroom dimly lighted by the slant of the afternoon sun streaming
through a shade pulled to the sill. She lay on the bed with the sheet
clutched over her breasts with both hands, her head turned to
stare silently at me as I inched toward her, holding my breath.

I read no expression on her pale face beneath the sandy hair
damp near the roots. Her hair was as shaggy as a cocker spaniel's
and her eyes were big and dark and moist. I had an urge to sit on
the edge of the bed and pet her, just hold her in my arms and
comfort her.

"You're a sweet boy," she whispered, releasing the sheet and
reaching toward me.

I gazed at her fingers, seeing the same sight that had previously
repulsed me.

I swallowed hard, trying to overcome my queasy feeling.

When I stopped halfway from the door to the bed, she said,
"Well?"

Feeling a hasty grip capture my middle, squeezing nervously, I unfastened my belt, slid my pants down, and almost tripped before squatting to slide off my loafers. I hobbled to the bed, pushed off the pants, socks, and shirt. Before I could turn to her, she reached out and touched my sides, causing me to flinch.

"Are you okay?" she asked.

"Ye. . .yeah," I uttered.

When I shucked my underwear down my thighs, she ran her fingers down my hips, caressing.

I reached out and pushed the sheet down and touched her small breasts that barely rose to twin pink points. I touched them with the tips of my fingers, outlining the skin that was as white as a kitchen sink and almost as rigid.

I wondered what in the world Jake had told her. What lies and tall tales had poured from his lips, only he and she knew. I did not dare ask.

A breeze blew the shade, a crackling whisper and a cool breath dancing over us, and I shivered hopelessly and pulled the sheet down to her hips. I pushed my body up, balancing on elbows.

As her milky thighs squeezed together tightly, I reached down to touch the triangle of hair.

She opened her eyes wider, gazing into my face and asking, "Where's your rubber?"

"Rubber?" I said.

"You know what a rubber is, don't you?"

"Of course," I answered stupidly, but did not move.

"Well," she said, buckling her arms over her chest.

I stared up at the old rain-stained ceiling where gray-circled plaster peeled. I could not think. I had not thought about pro-phylactics. They had never entered my mind. I wanted to close my eyes and make her vanish. I wanted to be a hundred miles away. But we were not living in a comic book world. The goose-bumps that popped onto my flesh made me quiver, and I pushed myself up, pulled my underwear around my middle, and muttered, "I'll be right back."

The bedroom door closed too loud behind me. I tiptoed down the wide hallway. From the top of the stairs, I called out in a whisper, "Jake?" I waited. There was no reply. I stepped halfway down. In a louder voice, I called again.

From the living room, Morris's head poked out of the door anxiously. "You through already?"

"No. Where's Jake?"

"Jake," Morris hollered. "Skinny-butt wants you."

Jake came out from the rear of the house. Jeans hung below his navel. He skipped up several stairs. "You got any rubbers?" I asked.

"The chest of drawers next to the bed?"

I climbed the long stairs again. Staring into the maroon and navy paisley pattern of the hall rug, I tried to clear my mind. Isn't the first time supposed to be wonderful? Think of nothing but the business at hand, I told myself. Think about her, her body, her face, her legs. . . When you move to the bed, take her in your arms. Run your fingers through her hair. Kiss her. Be gentle. Be loving.

I opened the door.

She sat on the edge of the bed. She looked older. Her thin shoulders bent forward. In her hands she held a rubber between thumb and forefinger.

She turned her dirty blonde cocker-spaniel head and looked without wonder into my eyes, which I promptly closed. I prayed that she would lean forward and kiss it, but she didn't.

After she'd applied the rubber like a mechanic changing a tire, she hiked herself up, lay back, and spread her legs, staring up into the ceiling.

As I elevated myself over her prone body, I whispered, "Touch it," and she did. She wrapped her fingers around it and pumped.

Momentarily, she guided me into the warm valley between her legs, where, after several quick thrusts, I spent my seed and collapsed onto her. I rolled off, dressed silently, and started to leave. Before I got to the door, she said, "Hey." I turned anxiously to her. She held her right arm extended toward me. Dangling from her fingers was the used rubber. I returned and undraped it from her fingers, again noticing the dirt under her fingernails.

Downstairs, I asked Jake about Uncle Morris. Jake shrugged and shook his head and said, "I told him he couldn't."

I didn't ask why.

Jake offered, "She didn't want to."

"Oh," I said, and I left the house alone, feeling empty and sad, thinking about her big brown eyes that seemed even sadder to me now, now that I was by myself, listening to a train from somewhere arriving at the depot.

Three days later, Jake came by the house on his Harley. "Borrow your old man's car tomorrow, we'll go down to Big Sandy and pick up Angie and take her on a picnic."

"Why don't we go swimming and take along some soap?" I asked.

Jake gave me a look and shook his head. "You won't do, man. Some kind of Brillo nut."

"I just like my ladies clean, that's all," I said. It wasn't like I'd been running around with a bevy of country club beauties. I could count all the real dates I'd had all my life on one hand.

"Think you can do it?"

"I'll ask," I said, and left it at that, feeling skeptical.

Then he said, "Why don't you buy us some rubbers? I furnished last time."

I hesitated, then reluctantly agreed.

When I asked for the car, Daddy didn't hesitate. He threw the keys to me, said, "Drive careful, and don't do anything I might do," chuckled, and said, "You can drop me and Donnie Lee off at the golf course on your way to wherever. I've arranged for him to have lessons and I've got a card game." Mama lowered her book instantly, glanced toward him, then at me, standing at the door with the keys in my hand. "Where're you going?" she asked.

"Jake and I are gonna pick up a couple of people and have a picnic down at Big Sandy," I said.

"Thomas has a country girl friend," Donnie Lee said.

"I do not," I said.

Mama smiled pleasantly and said, "Y'all be careful."

After I dropped off Daddy and Donnie Lee, I pulled in next to Canty's Gulf station. I stood at the corner and looked both ways before I stepped into the men's room where I'd seen the machine on the wall but had never slid quarters into the slot.

I dug my fingers into the pockets of my jeans. I shook my head, gritting my teeth when I came up with only one quarter. If I went to Mr. Canty and asked him for change, he would surely know what I was up to.

Outside, in the bright morning sunlight, I pulled a bill from my pocket. In the little office, I picked up a Baby Ruth and handed Mr. Canty my dollar. Smiling, I took the change from him, leisurely unwrapped the end of the chocolate bar and bit into it. I ambled back around toward the men's room, looking at the pumps and beyond, seeing no one.

In the men's room, I dropped the uneaten bar into the waste can, inserted two quarters into the machine, and turned the knob.

Nothing happened. No package appeared. I poked my finger into the hole where the package was supposed to fall. I felt nothing.

I twisted the chrome knob again. This time I turned it harder, heard an almost silent click, released the knob, and a small celophane-wrapped square dropped into the opening.

I reached up, lifted it out between the tips of my thumb and forefinger. I was holding it, examining it with a feeling of accomplishment and brief sophistication, when the door opened and the round bespectacled face of Brother Will Armstrong, the preacher who had given me more guidance than any other human in my life, appeared with wide-eyed astonishment. I froze, instantly stricken, unable to move or speak.

"Thomas," Brother Will said.

I started to say something but only stammered. Wishing I could will away the package, I palmed it as quickly as possible, almost dropped it, then slid it into my pocket.

Without a word, I moved toward the door which he opened wider while he stepped back and allowed my exit.

In Daddy's car, I sat behind the wheel for a long moment, staring at the closed door of the men's room. Feeling totally foolish, I knew there was nothing I could say or do to make his disappointing look vanish. I knew there was no possible redemption. Try as I might, Brother Will's heavy eyes staring at me would remain in my memory.

I took a deep breath, ran my fingers into the pocket and felt the sharp corners of the small package, then started the car, backed out of the parking place, and headed toward Jake's.

Jake guided me through a labyrinth of clay and sandy roads until we pulled into a broad yard with two pickups parked next to the house and a Studebaker on blocks with its engine hanging by a rusted chain from the limb of a chinaberry tree. The paint on the car's body had been baking in the west Alabama heat so long it curled up away from the metal, turning the color of dried blood. Beyond the tree sat a skinny boy on his haunches, glaring at us through the bright sunlight.

"Who's that?" I asked.

"Her brother, I reckon," Jake said. Then he said, "Beep."

I glanced at him. Even I knew it was bad manners to blow your horn for someone—especially a young woman in her father's yard.

"Beep," he said again.

I pressed lightly on the horn. It barely sounded.

"Again," he said. "Harder."

Just then, the boy bounded up like a bullfrog. In a moment he was hidden behind the chinaberry tree. A moment later he peered around the trunk, gazing in our direction.

"What's he doing?" I asked.

I held my hands at the horn. I did not push.

"Who the hell knows," Jake said.

A moment later the screen door at the rear of the square-built framed half-painted house opened and she ran across the sandy yard.

Jake held the door open, and she squeezed in next to him.

She grinned and said, "Hey," and Jake squirmed around and let her straddle his right knee. She glanced toward me, flashing her gapped teeth, and I said, "Hey."

I backtracked and headed south on the highway bordered by high pines covered with layer after layer of thick green kudzu that seemed to squeeze the life out of everything it touched.

When I slowed I saw something creeping up on us in my rearview.

"Who's that behind us?" I asked.

They both turned their heads.

"Your brother got a vehicle?" Jake asked.

"Joe Bob's got an old beat-up motorcycle, but it won't run worth a flip," she said.

"That might be him," I said.

As I turned off the highway, the big-leafed kudzu provided thick shade and camouflage. Before we were twenty feet off the main road we were so thoroughly hidden from the view of any passers-by that, even if they were searching, they were apt to move on without ever seeing a sign of us. I slowed almost to a stop, waiting, but we saw no one behind us.

Although it was not yet ten on a sweltering July Saturday without a cloud in the sky, when I braked Daddy's Chevrolet under a sycamore draped in kudzu, we were in semi-darkness.

Opening the door and stepping out, Angie opened her arms and sang, "Whee! This is really. . ."

Jake said, "Weird?"

"Mysterious," Angie said. "Like we're in another world."

"It's like twilight all the time," I said. I had found the place several years ago when I had a pinto pony named Navaho. Daddy had pulled a horse trailer down to a farm south of here where we decided to keep Navaho before selling her. I rode the pony through the swamplands, exploring, and this became one of my favorite places to hide, to pull off my clothes and swim naked in the icy water of Big Sandy Creek, and to hold Navaho close and tell her all of my secrets, which at the time were many.

Angie drew close to Jake, clinging to his left arm, as they followed me down a slick pathway toward the dark water.

"It's spooky," Angie whispered.

"The sun will shine down through the kudzu leaves, filtered green with natural chloroform," I said. "That's what makes it so weird," I said authoritatively. We were in my world now.

"How do you know so much?" Angie asked. "How does he know so much?" she asked Jake.

"Thomas reads a lot," he said. "He knows a lot about shit like this."

I chuckled, trying to break the tension. "I know a lot about a lot of shit," I said, trying to make it sound funny. It didn't.

"And he don't know shit about a lot of shit," Jake said.

I chuckled. He didn't have to say that, I thought.

But she laughed too, so it was okay.

Soon, both Angie and Jake had their clothes off and were stepping into the cold water of Big Sandy Creek, holding hands. She giggled and danced, picking her feet up high, splashing. Jake shivered and grabbed her and pulled her into the deeper water against her mild protest.

On the bank, my feet got tangled in my jeans. I almost fell, kicking off my loafers and shucking out of my tee shirt.

I followed them into the deeper water, feeling the tingle of cold goosebumps pop onto my skin. Jake's hands cupped her shiny white bottom. Her legs parted. Her slender thighs moved to surround his narrow hips that had begun to undulate naturally.

Even with the cold water washing against it, my penis hardened. I gasped.

My eyes riveted on them as he lifted her.

She glanced toward me, her eyes wide, and she said, "What're you looking at?"

"Thomas?!" Jake said.

I turned away, closed my eyes, and moved toward the mossy bank, hearing their sounds: heavy breathing, slushing the water with frantic movements, he slipping backward, falling into the water, she giggling, half out-of-breath, falling after him.

I did not turn toward them. Embarrassed by my own stupid erotic voyeurism, my brainless anxiety, watching them as if in a trance and being caught in my daydream, I did not now want to see them doing whatever it was they were doing. I gazed into the dark green woods where I thought I saw a movement and dismissed it as a deer or wild turkey or some other animal.

When a light touch weighed on my naked shoulder, I jumped. "What?" I said, turning.

She enveloped my body into her arms, rubbing her skinny body against mine, her hands pressing against my back, her midsection pushing against my middle. She opened her gape-toothed mouth and kissed me fully. I was astounded as her tongue flickered across my teeth and tickled my own tongue. When she reached down and touched my swollen penis, it exploded immediately. I felt hot tears suddenly welling up in my eyes. Angry disappointment filled me with the belief that I had once again blown my chance to be fulfilled.

My arms went slack.

But she did not relinquish her hold. If anything, it became more tense. She whispered, "That's okay." She splashed water on my body. She reached down and stroked, slowly, gently.

I heard myself gasp.

I lifted her up and out of the water and put her down on the mattress of moss. I knelt over her, looking from the sheen of her hair to the tips of her pointed toes. I gazed into the triangle of soft brown hair where her thighs parted. As I lowered myself into her, I said, "You're beautiful. You're totally and completely and irresolutely gorgeous."

As I felt myself sinking into her, as I heard her velvet voice say, "Yes, yes, yes," out of the corner of my eye I saw movement, heard someone shout, and knew something terrible was wrong.

But I could not stop.

My eyes were staring directly into her eyes, looking into something I had never seen before, lost in a world I had never before experienced. I did not stop, until a boot slammed against my side, cracking something. In an instant, I was knocked off the ledge. As I rolled, another kick slammed against my back.

I heard her cry out, first a slight animal-like eke in her throat, then a wailing sound of protest.

The heavy boot raked against the side of my head, tearing my ear and battering against my face, where blood exploded from my nose in a gush as a copper taste engulfed me.

As my eyes clouded and my stomach knotted, I grabbed my knees and held them tightly against my chest.

"Sonofabitch!" Jake spat. When I opened my eyes Jake was throwing his weight against my attacker, a red-faced, snarling hunk of pale skin and sinewy muscles, all tense and tight, flinging his lean arms toward Jake like a windmill out of control.

"Joe Bob, what are you doing?" screamed Angie as she fought to cover herself with hands, then scrambling on her hands and knees to gather her clothes and pull them onto her body. "Please! Please, Joe Bob, quit right now!"

But Joe Bob, who had the same light-brown hair as Angie and the same rawboned build, was kicking his heavy-toed paratrooper boots into Jake the same way he had slammed them hard against my right ear, which had come undone on the side of my head and was bleeding like a stuck hog.

I had backed up against a thick green bush, trying to hide my nakedness while my side and my head hurt with deep, gnawing pain.

Jake grabbed Joe Bob's boot that came up hard against Jake's ribs. Jake twisted, bulldogging Joe Bob to the ground, where he hit with a thud.

Seeing him hit the ground, I scrambled toward the pile of my clothes. Angie sat nearby, crying. I did not immediately pick up my clothes but jumped first into the water, thinking it might have some healing power to ease my pain.

It did not, but it managed to wash my body of the mud and blood.

When she saw my ear dangling from the side of my head, Angie screamed, "Oh, no! Your ear. . ." She pointed toward me.

I reached up, felt for the ear where blood spurted.

Angie ran toward Jake and grabbed his hands that were balled into fists, hammering down onto Joe Bob's prone body clamped on the ground by Jake's two knees.

When Jake looked dazed into her face, like he didn't even know who she was, she screamed, "We've got to take Thomas to the hospital right now!"

On the beat of her last word, Jake smashed his fist down into Joe Bob's nose.

Joe Bob, face smudged with dirt and blood, jerked his head to the side, and Jake's fist hit hard against a rock. "Goddammit!" Jake said, pulling his fist up with two knuckles skinned and bleeding.

"Jake! Come on! Leave Joe Bob!"

With his bleeding hand, Jake slapped Joe Bob's bony jaw. "You go home, boy," Jake commanded. "And forget what you saw out here. You understand?"

Joe Bob moaned, then rolled away quickly when Jake pulled off of his body.

With my clothes twisted onto my wet body and Jake's hand-kerchief held to my ear, they led me to Daddy's Chevrolet. All the way to the hospital I kept thinking: I'm bleeding on Daddy's front seat. He's gonna be mad. He's gonna ground me forever.

While Jake drove, Angie kept herself turned to face me. Her face was a picture of pure fright. She said, "You won't die, will you, Thomas?" and when I didn't answer, tears washed down her cheeks and her lips trembled and she said, "Oh, God, they're gonna arrest my brother for murder, if you die," while attendants in white jackets lifted me onto a stretcher and rolled me into the emergency room.

Behind a curtain, a nurse checked my blood pressure while another prepared a syringe which she squeezed into my arm. After that, I hardly felt a thing. In a fog, like my brain had numbed after Joe Bob had first kicked my head, I realized that a fresh-faced young doctor was working to sew my ear onto my head. Beyond the medical people I heard Jake and Angie talking excitedly. Jake was questioning her about Joe Bob and she was answering, "Hey, I didn't know he was following us. I had no idea!"

I had no idea how long I had been here or how long I would stay. After a while, their voices faded. In their place were the nervous sounds of Mama saying, "Will he be okay?" and Daddy saying, "Who did this?" and nobody answering either of them.

After an orderly wheeled me up to a room, my brain still floating a half-foot above my head, Mama and Daddy came through the door saying it looked like I had been run over by a Mack truck.

When I asked about Jake, Daddy said, "I ran the little bastard off. You've got no business messing with pure-dee trash like him," and Mama said, "Who was that girl?"

I just stared up into their faces, saying nothing, feeling like laughing, floating.

About a week later, I was sent home. My brain settled back down into my head, although it felt like it was twisted on wrong. My ear was swollen and the twenty-eight stitches looked like black tracks against the red skin.

When I asked him about Angie, Jake said, "I ran that sorry bitch off."

"It wasn't her fault," I said.

He shook his head and said, "She knew that sonofabitch was following us. She knew it all the time and didn't say a damn word."

After it got white-hot and sticky in mid-July, I couldn't help but think about her. I'd awaken early in the heat and lay in my bed and picture her and play with myself until I made a mess under the sheets. I made up my bed every morning, and Mama said she thought I was truly growing up, the way I was suddenly keeping my room neat.

I caught the bus to the AG&S depot and walked to Jake's Uncle Morris's house. The old man came to the door and stared at me through the screen. "I ain't seen the boy or the girl," Morris said. I could hear movements somewhere in the house. I turned and walked across the street and stood in the shade of an oak tree and stared at the house, waiting. About an hour later, the brown-skinned woman named Maggie came out the back door and walked toward the street. Before turning onto the sidewalk, she looked over at me and asked what I was waiting for. I shrugged, and she said, "You boys better watch y'all's asses. Ol' Morris ain't been the same since y'all brought that little ol' skinny white whore to the house and let him get hisself a sniff. Ever since, he ain't been worth killing. Walks around talking to hisself, saying he's looking for his nephew's woman. Woman hell! She ain't nothing but a sniveling little bitch. That's what she is!"

Back home, I moped around, trying to stay in the air-conditioning which Mama said was bad for our health, but I thought it was better than burning up in the hundred-degree weather. I tried to think of something to do, but couldn't. When I thought, I thought about Angie, and that just ran me to the bathroom, trying to relieve the awful ache.

On the phone, I told Jake, "I really feel bad about Angie, the way we dumped her and all."

"And you damn-near getting killed by her crazy brother?" he said.

"He was just mad," I said. Then I added, "I'd probably do the same, if I had a sister."

"But you ain't got a sister and neither do I. So we don't have to go acting crazy, just because she's opening her legs to every Tom, Dick and Harry."

"How do we know that?"

"How do you think I met her?" Jake asked. "She was putting out to Bill Dillard, and he told me, and then he gave me her telephone number, only it wasn't free."

"What'd you pay him?" I asked.

"One dollar. I gave him one dollar, and he gave me her number and told me to talk sweet to her and tell her I was a good Christian and she'd do anything I wanted. Then, after I told her, I told her you were a better Christian than me."

"That's really great, Jake." I felt totally exasperated. Not only was my ear swollen the size and shape of an eggplant, my insides were queasy with the thought of her. Now, to find out I had been represented as a card-carrying Christian, I felt even more mixed up than ever before.

"Well," I said, "the one thing you can do is give me her telephone number."

"For a dollar," he said.

"A dollar? After everything we've been through?"

"You don't expect me to take a loss, do you?"

"Jake!"

He produced the number from a worn piece of cardboard stuck behind the old rubber he kept in his imitation leather billfold. "Now, what are you going to do with it?" he asked.

"Call her," I said.

"Thomas, are you a total damn fool?"

"I have to," I said.

When I called I heard her brother or her father say, "Hello," and I just stood there in the hall of our house and said nothing. When he said, "Hello," again, an edge of anger in his voice, I hung up.

I tried to busy myself to make the time pass quickly, but fifteen minutes seemed forever, pacing back and forth from the kitchen to my room, glancing at the idle telephone each time I passed.

It was early the next day before I listened to the rings and heard her say, "Who is this?"

"Angie?"

"Yeah. Thomas?"

"Yeah."

"Has it been you who keeps calling and hanging up?"

I hesitated.

"I thought so. You or Jake. Y'all must be crazy. If Joe Bob figures it out, he'll tell Daddy, and the two of 'em are liable to skin you alive."

"Did Joe Bob tell. . ."

"No!" she interrupted. "He didn't, and he's not going to, but you better just quit calling here."

"I want to take you out on a date."

She said nothing.

"I'll take you to church."

"Church? What church?"

"My church. Covenant Presbyterian. Brother Will's the best preacher I ever heard."

"He's the one that invited the colored to his church," she said.

"That's right. He announced church is a place for all people to worship."

"He must be crazy."

"He's a wonderful man," I insisted.

"Well, he might be. But why on earth would you want to take me to church? Haven't you had everything you want from me? Haven't you been able to do everything you want to do? Usually a boy just shuts up and goes away, after he's got what he came after." She was talking low, whispery, and fast, like she wanted to pack everything into this conversation.

Finally, after she finished, I said, "Well, I'd just like for you to go with me to church, that's all."

"Do you feel guilty or something?"

"Well. . ."

"I thought so."

The phone suddenly slammed down onto the receiver.

I waited a few minutes, dialed her number again, and Joe Bob answered.

I swallowed hard, then said, "May I speak to Angie, please?"

"Who is this?"

I said my name in a nervous jitter.

Then I heard silence.

"Hello?" I inquired.

No one answered.

After a moment, Angie came on the line again. "You are crazy!" she said.

"Well?" I said.

"Well, what?"

"I'll pick you up at ten-thirty Sunday morning."

When I went to the door of the house in the middle of a field of sand, Joe Bob opened it and glared into my face with a sullen damp-eyed gaze. "Your ear's gone down," he said.

I glanced around the front room with its crippled old sofa that sagged to the right, an easy chair with faded cushions with the stuffing poking out the edges, and a table covered with red-and-white-checked oil cloth. Over the sofa hung a picture of the Last Supper with Judas leaning toward Jesus, who had a bright glow around his head.

When Joe Bob didn't ask me to sit, I stood with my weight on my right foot, then shifted to my left. I clinched my teeth, asking myself why I had done this crazy thing, knowing that Angie was right about my mental state of mind. I wanted to turn and run out of there that instant.

As I shifted my weight a third time, Angie came out of the back of the house wearing a knee-length dress with a floral print. It came up to her neck and had short puffed sleeves.

At the car, where I opened the front door for her, she said, "Mama made me this dress back in the spring."

"It's pretty," I said.

After I settled under the steering wheel, I looked over at her and admired the new look. Her hair was more blonde than it had been the first time I'd seen her. It glowed, like Jesus in the picture. Her fingernails were long and had been painted a pale cream color. She had on a touch of pink lipstick that made her lips full and perfectly shaped. After the car cleared the dusty drive past the Studebaker body hanging from the chinaberry tree, she slid across the seat until her thigh touched mine. I breathed deeply and turned to her with a smile. Her body emitted the strong flavor of Ivory soap. "You sure look pretty," I said.

"Do I?"

"You do," I said, and in a sudden flash, like lightning across the sky on a clear day, I relaxed. "You sure do," I said, and I lifted my arm and slid it around her shoulders and pulled her closer, where I could smell her better.

B l o o d K i n

W hen my father shot Uncle Wheeler, Daddy declared it self-defense by reason of insanity. Uncle Wheeler swore he would kill Daddy, who gave himself up to the sheriff, who knew precisely what to do: admit Daddy to Bryce Hospital for the mentally ill for observation. Since the doctors there had observed him before, they knew what to look for in Daddy's behavior.

My father, Harold Leland Reed, was tall but thick through the middle. He had a long face with a narrow chin marked with a jagged albino scar down the left side, disappearing under the chin. It was easy to imagine a broken beer bottle slicing through the skin in a barroom brawl or a rusty blade tearing at the flesh in revenge by a jilted lover. When I asked how it happened, he grinned slightly off-center and said he'd tell me some day.

Perfectly cut white hair curled high in a shiny pompadour atop his narrow widow's peak above his high Cherokee jaw-bones. His voice was deep and melodious, like a bass singer in a gospel quartet. He liked to talk about his Indian ancestry, but I questioned its authenticity, just as I wondered about many of his stories brought home from the road, where he lived most of the time.

He was a traveling salesman of barber and beauty supplies, and he loved the business. Mama said Daddy liked leaving home more than being there. Now and then, however, I'd catch an agonizing look in his eyes as he picked up his suitcase on

Monday morning. He took longer and longer getting ready to leave. Sometimes he got to Hargrove Road and turned around and came back, saying he'd forgotten something. He'd come through the front door and look around the living room, blunder through the kitchen where Donnie Lee and I would be finishing our cereal, then he'd go into the back bedroom where Mama was straightening her hose. He'd look around the bed and say he was sure he'd left something. Mama said she didn't know what. Then he'd come back into the kitchen with a blank look on his face and would work up a smile and say, "You boys want a ride?" Donnie Lee usually accepted and I'd choose to ride with the Jenkinses who lived up the street and had a son my age, Junior Jenkins, who was runtier than I and already had a bad complexion and tried to cover his face with his hands whenever he could. That was when I was thirteen, when Daddy was beginning to feel that he was losing me and I began feeling like I knew just about everything there was to know in this world. Nobody could tell me anything and make it stick.

By the time I was fifteen, I hated the fact that neither my father nor my mother had graduated from college. As far as I was concerned, Daddy was dumb as a garden hose. Mama was the smart one; at least she'd gone to night business school. When I was sixteen, Mama was assistant administrator of the new hospital and was bringing home more money than Daddy.

When we were little, Donnie Lee and I occasionally traveled with him in the summertime . We loved taking off from our house on Monday morning with our bag packed. Daddy made a big to-do about it, said we were his assistants on the road. For the first leg of the journey, usually to the south into the Black Belt, he would talk up a storm while sucking on his constant

Kool cigarette that bobbed between his lips. When the ash would get too long, it'd just fall off onto his broad chest, which he'd automatically brush off at the first stop. He'd tell us about where we were headed. "Down here at Greensboro, we're gonna visit with old man Aaron Kohn, a German Jew who came to this country forty years ago with nothing but his name. Now he's a rich merchant with a furniture store, a fine home, a farm where he raises beef cattle, and has educated three daughters. Miss Edna Till's Beauty Shoppe is at the end of Main Street. She does more business than lots of shops twice its size in towns twice as big."

Between his rambling sentences, Donnie Lee squeezed in a question or two, trying to get a bead on exactly what Daddy was talking about. "Are they related?" Donnie Lee asked, when Daddy stopped long enough to light a new Kool off the butt that had lost its ashes.

"Who?" Daddy said.

"Mr. Aaron Kohn and Miss Edna Till?" Donnie Lee asked.

"No, why would you ask that?" Daddy threw him a wondering look.

"Well, you put 'em together like they're related."

"They both live in Greensboro, and it's a small town," Daddy said.

After Daddy introduced us to Mr. Kohn, who was short and had a big nose and ears that stuck out the side of his head, Donnie Lee said, "Where do German Jews come from?"

Mr. Kohn laughed while Daddy shuffled and said, "Why, Germany, of course," and Mr. Kohn said, "You've got an inquisitive boy there, Harold."

Donnie Lee was that way: he wanted answers to the questions in his mind. And he didn't mind asking them.

Back then, Donnie Lee and I enjoyed riding hour after hour with Daddy, listening to his tales. If we rode through northwest Alabama, he told about the outlaw Rube Burrow and his gang, a bunch of railroad robbers who jumped trains and robbed payrolls bound for coal mines where companies from up north worked convicts and children, paying them next to nothing.

"How little were the children?" Donnie Lee asked one time between Dora and Cardova.

"As young as five years old," Daddy answered.

"Same age as me," Donnie Lee said.

"They'd send 'em down in the little narrow caverns where nobody else could go, let 'em check out whether there was any deadly gas trapped in those holes."

"What'd happen if there was any gas?" Donnie Lee asked.

"At best, they'd get sick and start coughing and throw up. At worst. . ."

"Ugh!" Donnie Lee said.

"I believe I like Rube Burrow best," I said.

"They called him the Robin Hood of the South," Daddy said.

"Why?" Donnie Lee asked.

"He robbed from the rich mining companies," Daddy said.

"Did he give to the poor?"

"I doubt it," Daddy said. "But legend says he gave gold and silver to the families of little children who died in the mining shafts."

"Who's 'legend'?" Donnie Lee asked.

"You ask too many questions, boy," Daddy said, a chuckle ringing in his words.

"Well?" Donnie Lee said.

"Legend is what's been told by those who probably didn't know for sure what actually happened in the first place," Daddy said.

"There's a lot of legend around," Donnie Lee said.

"That's for sure," Daddy said.

He lit another Kool and let it dangle from his damp lips.

By the mid-fifties, Daddy became a gin-rummy player and a raconteur of some notoriety between bouts of depression that landed him in the state hospital for the insane with more and more frequency. He might have been crazy, but he was never without cunning or imagination.

Once upon a time long ago he told us about serving in the army during World War II in New York. Donnie Lee wanted to know what kind of fighting went on there. Daddy ignored his question and told about seeing Frank Sinatra at the Paramount. One of the singer's teachers from high school had become a friend of Daddy's in the army and had received tickets to the show. Daddy went along, and late that evening they had a martini with Sinatra at the bar in the Waldorf-Astoria Hotel.

"What's a martini?" Donnie Lee asked.

"Four-fifths devil's juice mixed with a drop of heaven's honey," Daddy said with that little grin playing at his lips, just above the white scar. "It's as sweet and satisfying as a movie star's kiss."

"How many movie stars have you kissed?" Donnie Lee asked.

"I've had Rita Hayworth on this arm and Betty Grable on this one. I've had Jane Powell for breakfast, Ann Sheridan for lunch, and Marlene Dietrich for a seven-course candlelight dinner," he bragged.

Of course, this kind of talk came only when it was just the three of us in his car. Once when we got home at the end of the week, Donnie Lee excitedly told Mama about one of Daddy's tales. She just looked around at us and said, "Well, sometimes your daddy just talks too much," and let it go at that.

Later, the names of Daddy's movie stars changed to Debbie Reynolds, Elizabeth Taylor, and Marilyn Monroe. And in the sixties to Terry Moore, Brigitte Bardot, and Donna Michelle, Playmate of the Year for 1964. He could tell you everything about Miss Michelle—from her bust size to the fact that she was a failed ballet dancer, which he said made her all the more charming. He claimed to know her from a three-day trip to Chicago when, he said, he stayed at the Playboy mansion as the guest of Hugh Hefner, whom he called "Hef."

The only thing consistent about Daddy was his unpredictability that kept the rest of us alert to any possibility. He loved quoting the Irish poet: "Consistency is the curse of the unimaginative," raising his long head and tilting it to the side in a dramatic pose.

When I was twelve he rode my pinto pony, Navaho, in the Thanksgiving parade, dressed in an all-black Lash LaRue costume with a black wide-brimmed hat and carrying a leather whip. He knew the cowboy hero was our all-time favorite. Mama sighed deep in her throat and turned away. All of her life she made major efforts to keep me and Donnie Lee from becoming "like him." Donnie Lee, who was eight, managed to pull away from her and run to the front of the crowd and shout, "Daddy! Daddy!" and by the time I pushed my way through the crowd and could see over the heads of other kids, Daddy had maneuvered Navaho to the street's curb, leaned over, lifted my brother, and swung him up, where Donnie Lee grabbed a hold around Daddy's middle.

Mama, standing forlorn and helpless, uttered, "Oh, Harold, you're so. . ." and she glanced down at me and sighed again.

They rode away, both grinning like idiots.

Daddy and Donnie Lee and Navaho showed up late that night, and the next morning Mama huffed around the house and announced that she would be seeing a lawyer. "You can prepare to be gone," she told Daddy as he slouched over a bottle of Coca-Cola, which he preferred to coffee.

"Aw, Myrtie," he started.

"Now, don't start sweet-talking me," she snapped.

"I wanted to show the boys what it's like to be a star."

"Harold Reed!" she said.

"You only get to be a star a few times in your life, honey."

"Harold!"

"Donnie Lee enjoyed the ride, didn't you, boy?" His deep voice sang, lilting with misunderstood motives. "You liked seeing your old Daddy playing the part, didn't you, Thomas?"

I nodded shyly. I was never quite sure when he had a joke on the edge of his mind and when he was dead serious.

"He did not," Mama said.

"You can see that he did, honey," Daddy insisted. "The boys liked it."

By now he was standing, pulling his shiny brown gabardine pants up a notch and straightening his shoulders. He moved to her slowly, like a dancer, raising his arms from his body like tender wings, beckoning, until he was standing within inches of her and she could not help but step into him, lifting her face toward him as he leaned to her and surrounded her with his arms.

I slid from the breakfast table and made my way through the house to my room, where I lay on the bed and pushed my face into my pillow and wept, not even knowing why I was crying.

When my cousin Billy Joe, Uncle Wheeler's oldest boy, rushed through the door red-faced and short of breath, asking "Where the hell's your old man?" I was sitting at the bar at Mack Johnson's place talking to Mack and Sueleigh Bell.

I shrugged and said I didn't keep up with Daddy any more than he kept up with me. We were estranged since he showed up on campus at the public reading of my short story that had won a composition award. Between paragraphs, he clapped and shouted: "You're number one! Go, kid, go!" My professor, haughty and handsome in his silk paisley ascot and tailored Harris tweed jacket, approached him, only to have Daddy encircle his shoulders with a long arm and breathe sour alcohol into his face.

"Papa swears he's gonna kill Uncle Harold," said Billy Joe, a sawed-off runt of a twenty-one-year-old whom Daddy pointed to when he was preaching the evils of smoking. "It is obvious that smoking three packs of Marlboros every day stunted Billy Joe Hassell's growth when he was no more than fifteen. He hasn't grown an inch since."

"He's probably out at the Oasis or the Meadowbrook Golf Club or in Bryce," said Sueleigh Bell, my on-again off-again girl friend. I was twenty-two and she was three years younger.

Taking deep breaths and panting, Billy Joe said, "I'm afraid Papa's gonna kill him, the way he is. You know Papa, Thomas."

I nodded. I knew Uncle Wheeler very well, having been coon hunting with him and his brother and his father, having accepted my first drink of corn whiskey from them six years ago, and having seen him with his KKK hood on (or, even more revealing, when he took it off). There was a time when I thought Wheeler Hassell was a fine and honorable man who could walk at a full-legged stride through the thickest woods or deepest swamp all night following a pack of hounds on the scent of a frightened animal, but after I saw him scaring the be-Jesus out of poor little Negro children whose only sin was the color of their skin, I had no respect for him whatsoever. I wouldn't piss on Wheeler Hassell if his pants were on fire.

"Uncle Harold said he shot Papa for the good of all mankind," Billy Joe said.

"That would-a been a blessing," Sueleigh Bell said.

"Amen," said Mack Johnson.

Billy Joe gave her a beady-eyed stare, then he gave me a mean look. "You ain't worth a ounce more'n your old man," he spat.

"That's fine with me," I said.

"Not only is he not worth two-cents, he can't shoot either. He pointed that gun straight at Papa's head from no more'n six feet and pulled the trigger, grazing the left temple, knocking Papa for a winding and putting him in a three-hour coma."

"Too bad he didn't hit him square between the eyes," Sueleigh said.

"You gonna let her talk about your kin like that?" Billy Joe asked. He was in training to be a brakeman for the Southern Railway and thought he was the smartest Hassell in the United States and our homeland of Ireland as well as the entire state of Alabama. Last fall he told me I was nothing but a little college shit who didn't know his hind-end from second base, and I told him I'd have to agree, since I was born into the Hassell family by way of my mother. He said that it was an absolute fact that my father was "crazy as a shithouse rat," and I also had to agree with that assessment. It obviously made Billy Joe mad as a stirred-up hornet when I agreed with him.

"She knows him," I said.

"After Uncle Harold shot Papa, he screamed, 'I done it in self-defense 'cause I'm crazy insane.' Now, what kind of argument is that?"

"Sounds like the argument was settled," Sueleigh said. A pretty little thing with strawberry blonde hair teased into a fluffy helmet, Sueleigh, whose family came from down around Dothan in the far southeastern quadrant of Alabama, was known among some of her friends as The Wiregrass Whip. Lean and tan, she had muscular short legs and a slender butt that could make a mattress bounce. Small well-formed breasts were the objects of many young men's lustful desires. When I first started dating her, after my friend Jake Sims picked me up at the depot in southside when I came home from the Big Apple on the Southerner half-drunk and full of myself, she told me, "You can play with my titties, but that's as far as you go." And she kept to her declaration for two months, until one night we were parked at the cutoff near the Rice Mine Road. The full moon was shining down onto her perfect pair and I dropped my face between them, kissing them as usual, feeling the tiny nipples grow hard between my teeth, and she squirmed and said, "Lord God, Thomas, you're the slowest human being who ever wore pants," bringing her little bottom up off the seat and raising her skirt to help, opening her legs to allow me entrance to "the pathway to heaven." Ever since that night, we were a compatible couple.

Sueleigh laughed again as she looked into my cousin's sharp knife-like face.

Billy Joe wheeled around on his heels, marched to the front door, twisted toward us, and said, "You will be damned sorry you shit on me, Thomas Morgan Reed." With that, he did a neat military about-face and slammed the door behind him.

"Sounds like the Hassells are sore losers," commented Mack Johnson.

"I'll drink to that," I said, and had another Bud.

Into his fourth Early Times and ginger ale, Mack Johnson was getting down to serious business while Sueleigh and I were sitting quietly side by side, looking into each other's face, not needing to say anything. I was exploring the creamy smooth planes of her cheeks, the matched crevices in the corners of her muddy brown eyes, the arched curls of her long dark lashes.

Mack Johnson was saying, "Now, if I finish the upstairs by next Saturday, put up two C-notes, you operate the poker game and cut the pot. . ."

"What poker game?" Sueleigh asked, just like a woman.

"Mack and I are partners," I started.

Two hours later, parked on the levee below the Country Club next to the Black Warrior River, Sueleigh pushed my probing hands away and twisted to face out into the night. Moonbeams flickered on the water like liquid silver. The river looked like a beautiful, magical place, where insects sang a repetitious sad song. We were not close enough to smell the putrid sewage, raw garbage and chemical waste that our town dumped into it daily. Once on a dare I jumped from the railroad trestle into the dark water. I came up with oily debris clinging to my skin. I smelled like a cesspool and itched for a week.

"I don't want you running a poker game," Sueleigh said, pouting.

"It'll be good money," I said. "Just a bunch of gumps, losing their money."

"You take after your daddy more and more every day," she said. I winced.

"It'll be dangerous," she added.

"Since when have you worried about danger?" I asked.

"It's something else, driving a hundred miles an hour over Thrill Hill or jumping off the railroad trestle. Poker's real trouble. You know that. It could lead to a lifetime of crime, deceit and even prison."

When I tried to touch her again, she pushed me away. Three nights later I started the game on the second floor of Mack's place at nine p.m. with me and five players: seven stud, two-dollar ante, pot limit, cutting the pot a dollar each round, house ante free.

Mack had been dead serious about our rules: I would stay only if I had a pair of jacks or better, three toward a straight or flush. No drinking on my part. It was all business. "Better your hand with the fourth card, or fold," Mack stated in the privacy of the cramped little kitchen behind the bar. His shaggy gray brows raised and his bloodshot eyes glistening, he said, "Got that?"

"Got it," I said.

"Repeat it," he demanded.

The first night went great. At one a.m. closing, I had one-hundred-and-eighty-five dollars, which we split over a beer. Sueleigh sat next to me as I counted our winnings, making two stacks, while Mack fetched my first Bud of the night. When I finished one dollar odd, Mack said, "You keep it. You earned it."

An hour later, Sueleigh said a gambler did better at his game when he remained chaste.

I said she was full of shit.

She shook her head. "I read in Reader's Digest where athletes take a vow of celibacy to make their minds and bodies react sharply at a high-tuned level."

"What the hell does Reader's Digest know?" I asked. "And anyway, I'm not an athlete."

"I watched you play. You were good. Really good. You raised Winston Gaines at precisely the right moment to throw him off-balance. He was too frightened to call because you played your cards exactly right."

"Bullshit, I had a full-house and could have beaten anybody at the table. If I hadn't played so quick, making a hard bet, he would have stayed, and Mack and I would have won another twenty or thirty on the hand. I screwed it up because I was so tense and tight."

Although I begged, she would not give.

All morning, I tossed and tumbled. The next night I didn't do as well as the first. Still, Mack and I managed to split a c-note and fourteen ones.

Back at the levee, Sueleigh turned into me and opened her arms and said, "I reckon you deserve a little," as my head dropped down to her small breasts and I reached up her dress to feel the welcome warm comfort of the pathway to heaven.

Halfway through Saturday night, one of the players dropped out after I won a hand with two big pairs. He shook his head and said, "Too much for me," and disappeared down the stairs into the sounds of Hank Williams and the Drifting Cowboys on the Rock-Ola. Ten minutes later, new footfalls sounded on the steps, coming up.

I glanced toward the opening and saw Daddy's white head and long face and joyful smile. "You think your little rawhide ass can stand a real player?" he asked in a guttural drawl.

"Daddy. . ." I started, shuffling the cards and glancing questioningly at the others.

"I'm just another player," he said.

"You. . ." I started again.

"I heard you were running a game," he said. "Word gets around. They say you're pretty good."

My stomach felt queasy as he pulled a straight-back chair from the table, scraping the legs against the bare floor.

"Seven stud, high card opens," I announced as I dealt. I dropped out of the first three hands although I held a big pair hidden on each. As I tried to keep my eyes from looking into Daddy's face, my insides rolled.

But the time came when I had eight, nine, ten of hearts on the first three, nine and ten hidden, and no seven or jack of any suit showing. Only one other heart appeared on the table. I called Daddy's five-dollar bet.

Then I drew the jack of hearts. My stomach tightened. As Daddy bet twenty, I knew I was in for the ride.

Four of us remained. I stared into his pair of kings. I was sure the third was among his hole cards. He probably held my king of hearts. The other two players had a pair of fives and an ace, seven of different suits.

My fifth card showed nothing. He caught a ten and the others an eight and another ace. The pair of aces bet twenty. I called. Daddy raised twenty. The fourth player studied his cards for a long moment. I wondered why. If he had not helped his fives, he should fold. He called. I called. The pair of aces called.

Nothing paired but my jack on the sixth. With only two hearts showing on the table—neither the queen nor the seven, leaving my straight flush still a possibility—I had to call and hope for a heart on the last card. The odds favored my catching a good one. The aces bet fifty. Daddy raised fifty. I called.

"Crazy little shit," Daddy uttered when I pushed chips into the center.

I squeezed the seventh card up and into my hand. I eyed it closely: queen of hearts. Jackpot!

The aces bet a hundred.

I called.

Daddy raised a hundred, growling, "If you can't do nothing but call, you ain't got no call."

I swallowed hard, my throat constricting nervously, gripping my cards between sweaty fingers. I knew my hands were shaking, although I had my elbows anchored on the table.

The aces raised back a hundred.

Two-hundred to me.

"What's the pot?" I asked, barely able to squeeze the words from my lips.

I counted five-hundred and pushed the stacks into the middle.

Daddy, still grinning, shook his head. He leaned forward and stared at the aces for a long moment.

Fold! I said to myself, wishing him out of the hand.

Then he looked down at my hand and shook his head again. The white zigzag across the left side of his chin quivered.

Fold! I thought again, hoping I could relay my telepathic message to him.

At that moment my first-cousin, Billy Joe Hassell, stepped out of the darkness of the stairway. "You goddamn sonofabitch," he muttered, and in the shadows of the single light that hung over the table I caught the glimmer of a gun-barrel pointed toward us.

"You bastard!" he snapped, and the snub-barrel revolver waved directly toward Daddy.

Daddy's smile held as he muttered, "What the hell are you doing, Billy Joe? You lost all your senses, boy? Them cigarettes done smoldered your brain?" As he spoke, his ever-present Kool bobbed up and down.

"I'm gonna kill you," Billy Joe snarled.

"I should-a gone ahead and killed your daddy when I had the chance," Daddy said.

"Shut up!" I ordered, glancing toward him.

I rose and stepped toward Billy Joe, my hands outstretched as though I were begging. "You know he doesn't mean it, Billy Joe," I said. "Daddy would-a killed Uncle Wheeler, if he'd really wanted to. All you're gonna do is get your own ass in a world of trouble."

"Sit down, Thomas," Billy Joe said. "I ain't got no truck with you. But I'm gonna kill shit out of your old man."

I kept my hands outstretched. "It's my game, Billy Joe. Cousin or not, I can't let you interrupt it." I stepped easily toward him, walking gingerly, like the floor was glass.

As I looked at it, the small barrel of the gun got bigger and bigger.

Behind me, Daddy said, "Sit down, son."

"Daddy, don't you move," I said.

As I inched closer to Billy Joe, tears streaked down his nicotine-browned cheeks. His small eyes were red-rimmed and full of damp fright. Fingers that were stained as brown as his face shook uncontrollably.

"Put it down, Billy Joe," I whispered. "Whatever Daddy did to Uncle Wheeler, we can't solve it like this."

"It ain't Papa I come about," Billy Joe said through clinched teeth.

As I reached to him, my stomach squeezed up into my esophagus. I took hold of the gun's greasy barrel and twisted it sideways. He let go without a struggle and I quickly dropped it into my pocket. I swallowed a gulp of air, feeling the immediate need to pee.

Billy Joe stepped to me, collapsing into my arms, tears overcoming him as he grasped my shoulders desperately.

"Let me at the little bastard," Daddy said behind me.

I raised my hand and motioned Daddy back.

"He's been screwing my little sister," Billy Joe cried into my ear.

I pushed him back and stared into his blood-veined eyes and knew he was telling the gospel. "Mandy?" I asked.

"Yeah," he whimpered.

I pivoted toward Daddy, thinking I would hit him. I could see my little cousin Mandy Hassell, freckle-faced, country ugly, fat, shapeless, and half-witted.

"She's eighteen, but she's dumb as a post and don't know doodley-squat about anything," Billy Joe said.

"She fucks like a mink," Daddy said.

I glanced toward him with a look of pure disgust. "God damn, Daddy, she's your. . ."

"She ain't no blood kin," he said, looking around with an innocent expression masking his face. "Well, she ain't," he said.

I stepped toward him, my fists balled, my brain fuzzy, then I stopped, wondering if I would turn out to be just like him.

"Get out of here," I ordered.

"What about. . ." He looked down at the table, the cards, the huge of chips covering the middle.

"Look at my hand," I said, although neither he nor the aces had called my five-hundred-dollar bet.

He flipped my three down-cards, showing that my straight flush had filled.

I heard him say, "Shit," under his breath.

Tom Hendrix, who had been holding aces full, said, "I'll be god-damn."

Daddy started down the stairs, then turned back and stared at me, his eyes glistening. His voice pinched, he said, "I didn't do anything she didn't want me to do."

I started toward him, but I stopped. I held myself. I breathed deep, hearing my own heartbeats.

Daddy turned and walked away, down into the darkness, his sound of his footsteps diminishing step for step, music rising behind him as he opened and slammed the door into the barroom.

After a while, after I went to the bathroom and Billy Joe washed his face, I raked in the pot. Later I shared the take with Mack. It was our biggest of the week. But my pockets felt heavy with Judas' gold pieces weighing me down.

Having a beer at two a.m. with Sueleigh, I told Mack that my poker days were over. "My nerves aren't strong enough," I said.

"Hell, boy, with an old man like yours, you've got nerves of steel—a regular Superman," he said, but he was glad to take his winnings and be thankful that no real violence had happened.

Late in my junior year at the University of Alabama I visited Daddy, who'd been locked up for six months and had just been moved to a clinical psychology ward where he was undergoing analysis.

After a lonely lunch with Mama, she said that I should go see him. "He asks about you, and I tell him you're writing, and he wants to know when you're going to write him, and I tell him you're writing short stories and poems and plays and things like that."

The bright afternoon was heavy with the fragrance of Tuscaloosa flowers: magnolias and honeysuckle and oaks and bitterweeds and clover. The smell of paper mill waste tinged the air. The grounds at Bryce had been mowed, adding the flavor of fresh cut grass to the atmosphere. White Camellias dotted rich forest-green bushes. All of the growth was clipped to a sharp freshness and appeared orderly, like the lawn of a rich man's mansion.

I walked into a sunny drab dayroom with large family-style tables and benches surrounded by gray walls. I stood next to wire-mesh-covered windows and looked out onto neat broad yards. He entered through a plain door that matched the walls. He took three steps and stopped and stared at me with absent eyes. I'd never seen his eyes so lifeless.

"Thomas," he whispered, unsure. His airy voice filled the room. He gazed around in wonder. "I met your mother here last week," he said.

I nodded. "She told me," I said.

"Mama said you were writing, but you must not know my address."

I swallowed. It hurt, just looking at him, seeing him so pale, the zigzag scar blending with the sallow complexion, losing its mysterious allure. It had never known such anonymity.

"What do you do. . ." I started. I wanted to be perfectly logical with him. I wanted to let him know I didn't think he was crazy. I wanted desperately to reassure him.

"I walk," he said.

"Walk?" I asked.

"Anything wrong with that?" he asked.

"No, sir."

"No need to be curt with me."

"I'm not." I waited. I closed my teeth on the tip of my tongue. My mouth tasted strangely metallic.

"I walk out there," he said, moving toward the window with its wires crisscrossing the thick glass. "In my gardens. The servants keep it trimmed neat and pretty. It is neat and pretty, don't you think?"

I nodded.

He turned and his face twisted into a frown. His face flushed and the scar found its whiteness, like a streak of silver lightning in a darkening sky. "You don't believe me?"

"Yes, sir," I said. "I believe you."

"I don't just walk in little circles, going around and around, like some of the crazies in here." He chuckled, nodding, his eyes twinkling. "I walk with purpose. Sometimes with my dog. Sometimes alone." He gazed out the window.

I looked over his shoulder, through the window, beyond the wire mesh.

He turned to me and stared into my face, eyes damp with sudden tears. "You don't believe a word I'm saying, do you?"

I nodded. "Yes, sir, I do."

"No, you don't."

"I do." I tried to be very emphatic, very positive.

"You do not," he said. "You never have believed me. Never!" sharply. "I'd tell you things, but. . ."

"Daddy. . ." I started.

"You don't believe me," he said with resignation, his lips trembling.

I said nothing. I stared into his red face that was once again fading to a pale shade of gray.

"See," he said.

"What?"

"You don't believe me."

"But I do."

"You don't. I can see it in your eyes. You don't believe a word I say. It shows all over you. You came here to mock me, your own father, a man who has given you everything, a man who has cared so much for you and your mother and your brother. You and her, you never come to see me. Donnie Lee, he comes every day. He walks with me out there in the sunlight, between the Camellia bushes, smelling the sweet breath of spring. It is so delicious. He comes and walks and talks. He cares."

I started to say: Daddy, Donnie Lee's in Texas. He got a divorce and moved away because he couldn't stand it here. He's married again and has three kids by his new wife. He's afraid of you and won't let you near his children. He begged his ex to join him. He swore he'd never come back here. He had to live in a place as big as Texas.

Daddy crumbled onto a bench, his shoulders sagging, his face as gray as the walls, his arms a fraction of their once-muscular size. His arms folded on the table and he lowered his head into their nest and wept, his shoulders shivering.

When I touched him, he winced, sat up straight, blinked his eyes dry, cocked his head, and stared into my face. "Get out of here," he said. "Leave me alone. You don't need for you to come here and make fun of me. You and your mother." Then he said louder, "Go."

As his single word echoed through the room, two men in mint-green uniforms strode through the gray doorway and stepped to him and put their hands under his arms. They lifted gently, and he went with them, his feet moving mechanically. He turned to the one on his right and said, "Let's go walking," as the door opened and they moved through it.

I drove through the last of the waning sunlight to the campus, parked in the lot behind the library and made my way to the third floor where I entered the conference room with the long mahogany table. At the far end sat the handsome man with the big head and the long Roman nose and the neatly clipped iron-gray mustache. His wide shoulders were fitted into the once-stylish tweed jacket, now threadbare. "You're late, Mr. Reed," he announced, accusing.

"I'm sorry, sir," I said. "I've been visiting my father."

"Your father?"

"Yes, sir."

"I met him once," the professor began. "He was a most interesting man. Yes, a most interesting man," he said thoughtfully. "I think I shall never forget him."

I ' l l   F l y   A w a y

On Friday morning, Mama called.

Her words were soaked with despair. "He's not doing well, son. They had to restrain him yesterday. He tried to hurt himself." Daddy had tried to leap from a third-floor balcony of Bryce Hospital for the mentally ill. He decided he could fly. For years he had wanted to.

After his first stay at Bryce's, I drove him to the Meadowbrook Golf Club. He had a Schlitz and watched his friends play gin-rummy. He asked me to drive around through the neighborhood before going home. Smiling, he said, "Wouldn't it be great to open your wings and take off, like a bird."

After Mama called, I drove the hundred miles north to Tuscaloosa.

Entering the house, I looked around at all I had known, but it was foreign, heavy with the perfume of childhood, strains of heartache, echoes of emotional poverty.

I put my bag on the single bed. Above, an Alabama Crimson Tide pennant on the wall. Below, a faded photograph of me and my old friend Jake Sims at Boy Scout camp. Jake's eyes were too happy to have been burned alive in Vietnam while his platoon listened to his mournful cries. On the bedside table I was a stranger in a white dinner-jacket, holding Mary Russell Simmons on my arm at the senior prom. She was too pretty and pert to have been tortured by the big C that spread through her body until she withered away to nothing by age twenty-four.

Hearing the sound of a car door slam, I tore myself from memory.

At the front door, her voice caught in her throat. Then she managed, "Harold's dead." I opened my arms and folded them around her, hearing her whimper, feeling her tears against my neck. "Oh, Mama," I said, and she shook like a dead leaf in the wind.

After a while, we sat at the kitchen table, and she told me how he'd taken too much medication. She frowned and shook her head, "How can you do that in that place? It looks like they'd keep a close watch on...on the patients."

I nodded. I felt drained, void of feeling. Whatever had been no longer existed, like the lady next door whose name I could no longer remember, a person who had meant so much when the world thought of me as a boy. How can you forget the name of someone whose picture you carried in memory for years? Whose body and spirit made you ache in the middle of the night? But her name, and even most of the memory, was gone.

After Mama called my brother, Donnie Lee, who was living somewhere in the Texas Panhandle, I found myself saying that Daddy had gotten lost from the real world.

Mama stared at me through filmy red eyes. Her brow wrinkled and she shook her head and, in a scratchy high-pitched voice, said, "His constitution was always weak."

I looked at her, wondering. My father had had the constitution of a bulldog. He'd eat anything. On a week-long sales trip through Alabama's Black Belt, where he called on every barber and beauty shop, my brother and I watched him eat Possum-brand sardines out of a can and a wedge of rat cheese cut from a giant hoop and pickled pigs feet that made my skin crawl when he sucked between the toes. He washed it all down with an ice-cold Dr. Pepper. On the way to the next town, Daddy smoked a pack of Kools with his left arm, burned red, stuck out the window of his year-old Chevrolet.

I awakened from a deep sleep to look around the darkness of the strange bedroom, feeling like a giant in a land of midgets. I'd overgrown the narrowness of the bed, the low ceilings, the room, the house. The apartment I shared with roommates in Montgomery was huge, cut from an antebellum mansion, with eighteen-foot ceilings and gigantic rooms, and I had a king-sized bed.

Wide awake, I suddenly remembered the woman next door, Edna Williams, and I saw the outline of her panties tight against the thin material of her housecoat as she leaned forward on tip-toes to pin her husband's sleeveless undershirt to the clothesline. When she winked at me, her eyes bright with a promise, I shivered and my insides weakened.

The next morning, drinking coffee, I asked, "Do you know whatever became of Edna Williams after she moved from next door?"

"Why, no," Mama said. "I don't know whatever happened to her. She and her little girl moved off somewhere. I heard she got married again."

"I was just wondering," I said.

I tried to remember the child. I only remembered the woman and her backside and her winsome wink, and I remembered the awful sound of her screaming, "Noooo!" through a rain-soaked morning after she heard that her husband, Ralph, had been killed in a car wreck. Mama had told me she was pregnant, making the tragedy even worse. After that, the memory of her was only a vague recollection.

On the way to the funeral home, I said, "I was thinking about Edna Williams last night. I was thinking about the terrible way she kept crying out, 'No,' all morning after her husband died. It was so sudden."

"Like with Harold," Mama said.

I thought: No, not like Daddy. Daddy's death was not sudden. Daddy was gone a long time ago. Looking at Mama staring out the window and hearing her almost inaudible sigh as I turned into the parking lot, I knew she had not seen Daddy as I had. I had given up on him long ago. Until yesterday, she held hope for his emergence once again as the man she'd loved and married. I had moved on to a new time and a new place.

We made it through the morning with the funeral director. Back home, a lady from the church brought platters of food: a half-dozen freshly thawed casseroles, two different kinds of deviled eggs, potato salad, green-bean salad, English pea salad, cheese-and-raisin salad, a sackful of yeast rolls, and a mountain of fried chicken. I was halfway finished with my second drumstick when the front door burst open and my brother's voice called, "Am I at the right place?"

Mama rushed out and threw herself into his arms. "My baby," she uttered, kissing his neck as he lifted her from the floor. "Mama, Mama, Mama," he said.

He grabbed my biceps and squeezed, saying, "Brother," his voice breaking as he gazed into my face, seeing my aging as I saw his: tiny crowsfeet fanning from the corners of his eyes, deep furrows lining his long forehead, a girth that had expanded from a youthful athlete's narrow, hipless middle to a beer drinker's gut, and a hesitancy in his speech, as though he'd been thinking about this moment over the past five-hundred miles, and now didn't know quite what to say. He was my brother and her son, but there was an unfamiliarity of growth, an absence of three years, a flash in time when years of love and loss and sorrow and happiness all filtered down to now.

We stood there, touching, feeling far apart and uneasy, grasping for each other across a sea of quiet turbulence. "Mama," Donnie Lee said. "I'm sorry." He ducked his head and buried his face in her narrow shoulder and thin neck.

"I know, baby," Mama said, and held him while I stood stone-still until he raised his head and dug a handkerchief from his pocket.

"I've got some coffee made," Mama said.

"There's piles of food," I said.

"I just want to hit the bed and sleep like a zombie," Donnie Lee said. Then he blinked and said, "There's nothing we have to do, is there?"

"Not until tonight," Mama said. "Visitation from five to seven at the funeral home."

Donnie Lee glanced toward me and I nodded. "Wake me at four-thirty," he said, then disappeared into the house.

Mama and I sat in silence in the semi-darkness of the kitchen and sipped our coffee and listened to his snoring.

At four-twenty-five, I shook his shoulder. "Donnie Lee," I said. He mumbled something, pulled away, looked into my face. Recognizing, he said "Oh."

He swung his legs off the bed. He said, "I'm not Donnie Lee anymore. I'm just plain Don," then stumbled into the bathroom.

At ten-to-five, we rode to the funeral home. I drove. My brother sat next to me. Mama sat like a statue in the back. The first out of the car, she moved across the parking lot.

Don and I hurried to catch up.

Inside the room with muted lighting and piped-in music, we led her, like a waltz in slow motion, toward the open casket. She gasped a tiny breath deep in her throat. I felt her grip tighten as Daddy's profile came into view.

He did not look like himself. His features were too sharp: his nose too long, his chin jutting upward, his throat without wrinkles. His skin pale gray and wax-like.

From Mama's other side, Donnie Lee uttered, "Uh uh," in disbelief.

Then the faint light shone on the white scar zigzagging from the left edge of his placid lips to the bottom of his chin.

For the first time in years he looked peaceful.

"Daddy," I said.

Mama's grip tightened again.

"Daddy," Donnie Lee said, the same way I'd said it, but more lonely and desperate, seeking, searching, the second syllable breaking.

A shudder went through us like a wave of electricity. We quivered together.

When we felt the presence of others behind us, we parted.

I fetched a box of Kleenex, brought it to Mama, and Donnie Lee took a wad.

In the next hour, people came. Faces appeared in the door and floated toward us, mouthing words of grief, taking our hands, explaining themselves and how they knew Daddy. Kinfolks came from north Alabama where Daddy had been born and raised. Aunts and uncles and cousins we saw only at funerals or an occasional wedding hugged us and kissed Mama on the cheek. They shook their heads and looked sad. They were all sincerely empty and counterfeit in their grief.

A salesman who'd known Daddy years ago appeared at the door. I thought Mama was going to wilt. Donnie Lee and I grabbed for her, holding her. The man stepped to her and said his name. "He loved you so," she whispered, as he took her small body in his grip and rocked back and forth. Momentarily, she backed away and they held each other at arm's length, looking at each other through their tears. "Boys," Mama said finally. "This is Alva Gibbons, your father's best friend." I'd met the man once, out on the road with Daddy, but I never thought of him as Daddy's best friend.

Alva, a tall, bald man with a pink hew to his skin, cleared his throat and said, "We traveled together for years and years, meeting up at places like Greenville and Enterprise, Montgomery and Selma. I sold dry goods. Like Harold, my line fell short somewhere in the late fifties, and I had to move to selling cars." His eyes shifted back to Mama. "Ella and I still live in Anniston, and I sell for the big Chevrolet dealership up there. I haven't seen Harold in six, seven years."

"Harold was partial to Chevrolets," Mama said as she guided him toward the coffin. Moments later, he wept and Mama put her arm onto his shoulder.

Mama's cousin, Ray Hassell, appeared in the doorway like a magician. He smiled like he was considering a joke. A wiry man, slender and short, he had ruddy skin and a glint in his eyes. The last time I had seen him he was wearing a wide-brim hat cocked over his right eye, shading that side of his face. He had a thin mustache that clung to his upper lip. He'd been up at Granddaddy and Nanny's in the country at Samantha, a community where many of the Hassells were born and raised, where they hunted coons in the swamps and killed hogs in the winter and farmed corn and hay in the summer, made gardens, and got along like they'd gotten along since the first Hassells came over from the poor farmland of southern Ireland more than a century ago. Ray still had that Irish flare about him. No bigger than Mama, he didn't mope and drag his feet. He stepped spryly.

There was a sharp crease in his chocolate brown trousers. His yellow shirt was open at the collar. He wasn't ashamed of being the only man in the room without a tie. He stepped to Mama and gathered her into his arms and picked her up off the floor. "Damn, Myrt, you're still light as a cloud." Mama rapped Ray playfully on the shoulders with both hands. "Ray Hassell, you're a sight," she said. She hugged him and kissed his cheeks. "The wind's slapped your face," she said. And he said, "That's what happens when you're welding on a pipeline in the Alaska chills. It's cold as the devil up there."

"I thought the devil would be hot," she said.

For a moment, I thought she'd forgotten Daddy.

Instantly, she turned with Ray to the coffin. Ray said, "I sure hate to look at dead people. Folks always say how natural they look. But ol' Harold don't look natural at all. He was natural when he was stepping around, funning folks, playing tricks, and having himself a big time. When he was talking up a storm, conjuring a sale or two."

"Ray, you always had a way of speaking the truth," she said, gazing down into the container than held my father.

Momentarily, they turned back toward me and Donnie Lee. Mama eased away from her cousin. She greeted others. Several from the Elks Club came in and shook her hand. A woman from the church hugged Mama and glanced at Daddy. It seemed to me there was more disdain in her eyes than sympathy. She spoke to us. I shrugged. I didn't commit to her. I couldn't. Donnie Lee turned away.

Mama threw me a look.

Ray stayed. He sat in the corner. It seemed as though he was watching us, trying to determine something about us. As the evening wore on, I became more and more aware of his eyes.

At the end of the second hour we prepared to leave. Ray stayed with us. At the front door, Mama turned to Ray. "Do you have a place to stay?"

He nodded. Then, like an after-thought, he said, "Would y'all like to have dinner with me? I remember this place downtown, The Fish Basket, had fresh seafood brought up from the Gulf."

Mama glanced toward us. Neither of us uttered a sound.

"There's a world of food at the house," Mama said. "More than me and the boys could ever eat."

"You always liked shrimp, Myrt," he said. "Sauteed in garlic and butter."

For the first time in two days, Mama smiled. She glanced into our faces. "Boys?"

"Thomas? Donnie Lee? Wouldn't y'all like some shrimp or oysters? Maybe some red snapper from the sea?" Ray asked.

At the sound of his name, my brother glanced toward me. "Sounds fine to me," he said, holding the door open while Mama stepped out. Ray moved after her. I followed.

The Fish Basket was a storefront cafe down from the pool hall where Donnie Lee and I used to hang out, seduced by the staccato sounds of solid balls, the mechanical action of a tapered stick through powdered fingers, words peppered with profanity as the cueball struck at an angle that gave geometry a meaning.

Entering, the fragrance of strong herbs surrounded us. Even before we were seated against a wall covered with student art-work, fanciful abstracts of meaningless shapes, the light lifted the veil of sadness that had shrouded us. Mama's pale face brightened. Her eyes lightened. Her nose, too big for her face, flared with the rich smells.

Ray ordered a bottle of chilled chardonnay. Mama waved away the offer of a glass, but Ray told the waiter to put it down. "She may like a taste with dinner," he said, offhandedly.

Mama smiled, not protesting.

Ray and Donnie Lee and I raised our glasses. Ray offered a toast. Looking at Mama, raising his heavy steel-gray brows, he said, "Myrt, sure you won't have a taste with us? We're drinking to Harold."

Mama shrugged, holding her smile. "Well..." she said. "Just a touch."

Ray poured a taste.

She touched her glass to ours.

"Harold was one of the most alive people I ever knew," Ray said.

Donnie Lee and I frowned.

"Harold was light on his feet," Ray continued.

I noticed Mama held her glass to her lips. The liquid touched her lips, but she didn't swallow.

"For a large man, tall and big-boned, heavy through the girth, he walked like a dancer, barely touching the floor. When he talked, his words flowed. He was exuberant."

I nodded. I'd never thought of Daddy like that.

"Harold's words were never boring. They sang. They told a story. They hit the nail on the head. He never beat around the bush. He could-of been a songwriter, if he'd known music."

Between sips, my brother's eyes focused on our old cousin. I didn't think he knew Ray as well as I—and I had been with him only two or three times. When I was a kid, spending the night with Nanny and Granddaddy, Ray came with a frayed old pasteboard guitar case from which he'd extracted a cheap pawnshop instrument and played ballads and sang in brittle off-key notes. I remembered his voice, raspy and not-so-clear, singing in the night about a cowboy whose love was leaving and would never return. His was a plaintive voice remembered from more than ten years ago.

As Donnie Lee stared into his face, Ray said, "Harold was a poet. Small-town people knew him and loved him. Everywhere he went he spread a joyful view of the world. People loved to see him come."

"He was crazy as a lunatic," Don blurted.

Mama frowned, looking into her younger son's face in the bright overhead light, like she was seeing him for the first time.

Ray didn't disagree. "That's part of being a poet. He sees things different, from a different slant, not like ordinary people. Ordinary people are a dime a dozen. Harold was something special."

Don frowned, like he was staring into a carnival mirror that reflected distorted images.

"Blessed with a poet's vision, you're tortured without having the slightest idea what makes you the way you are."

"I think that's bullshit," Don said.

"Son!" Mama said.

"Well..." Don said. He looked toward me.

My eyes shifted back to Ray.

"Harold acted the fool sometimes," Ray said. "That too was part of his personality."

"He was a fool most of the time," my brother said.

"Your father loved the road," Ray said.

"That's why he left us all the time," Don said.

"He was eaten up with loneliness, driving on the highway by himself, every mile longer and longer. He got so lonely he tried to escape by coming home and being close to y'all, but finding himself fenced-in by what he had been doing all of his life: a traveling salesman. He didn't know anything else. His office was his car. He bounced from barber shop to beauty shop, bringing people a smile and a bright word. Folks knew him in every little town in his territory. They loved to see him coming. For a moment or two, his joy was theirs to share, before they went back to cutting or washing hair. Can you think of anything more monotonous? When he left them, he left his mark. Right now, all over small-town Alabama, people are missing him. They're thinking back on the memories of him, the story he told them the last time he visited, the picture of his sons that he painted for them.

"I rode with him a time or two way back. I'd come in from one of my trips out west. I'd have some time to kill. Back then, that's what I thought you did with time: kill it or while it away."

He took another swallow and poured more wine.

Don and I glanced at each other. He blinked away a tear. I felt one coming.

Mama held her glass out for another drop or two.

"I enjoyed my time with Harold," Ray said. "When we got back from a week on the road, I'd take the memory of his stories with me. His words kept me company many a-night.

"Sure, he was crazy." He grinned, showing teeth crooked from birth and yellowed from tobacco. "He was crazy in the best way I know: it came natural to him. Hell, you wouldn't be sitting here now, talking about him over a glass of wine, if he was a every-day Kiwanis Club asshole who attended church every Sunday and patted little children on the head and told mamas her little babies were cute. There was nothing hypocritical about your old man. Say what you will, he was a damned interesting guy."

"He thought he could fly," I said.

"What's wrong with wanting to fly?" Ray said.

"You can kill yourself," Don said.

"Or you can soar like an eagle, in your own way."

"He enjoyed talking about it," I said. I told them about the time he said he really wanted to fly.

Jovially, Ray said, "I bet that's what he's doing right now. I bet he's flying high above the treetops, hearing the wind sing in his ears. He's gliding along pretty as you please, belting out that old song, 'I'll Fly Away,' with the birds and the angels singing harmony."

Don gave him a skeptical glance but said nothing.

Mama nodded. A smile filled her face. "I'll drink to that," she said, lifting her glass. We all brought our glasses up and touched them with a resounding clink.

As we drank, I noticed that Don's scowl had not vanished.

Later, after we dropped Ray at his motel, after Mama went to bed, Don and I had one last nightcap.

We sat at the kitchen table. I leaned forward and stared into my brother's shaded face. His eyes looked tired, his face weary.

"How's Texas?" I asked.

"Like anywhere else," he said.

I was the one who stayed close to home. I was the one who always talked about traveling. I went to Mexico for the summer, to Greece for a short holiday, to London for a stolen weekend.

It was he who put miles and miles behind him to settle down with a new family in a new place, trying to escape this town, this house, this kitchen.

"That old man is still as full of shit as he was when we were kids," he said.

It took me a moment to realize he was talking about our cousin, Ray.

"Yeah," I said. "I guess he is."

Later, as I lay awake, thinking that I believed in Ray. I believed in his words, his bullshit. I believed in the idea of thinking you could fly, if only for a moment.

The next day, sitting next to Mama on the front pew, I raised my voice to sing with all of the congregation, "I'll fly away, oh glory, I'll fly away," our collective voice just as out of key as I remembered Ray's voice that night when he sang with the old guitar.

After Daddy was put into his grave and the preacher sprinkled dust onto his coffin, it was Don who pointed out that Ray had not made it to the funeral.

Mama said, "I don't reckon he could stand it."

Don looked at her, frowning.

I shrugged.

"Some folks just can't stand to attend funerals," Mama said.

"Then, why'd he come to begin with?" he asked.

Mama gazed at him incredulously.

That night, when we were alone again at the kitchen table, Don shook his head. "I don't guess I'll ever understand people," he said.

"How's that?" I said.

"Ray came all the way up here from south Georgia. He came all the way, two or three hundred miles, then he didn't bother to attend the funeral."

"Mama's probably right," I said.

"But he came all that way."

"He saw us. He saw Mama."

"You mean. . ."

"He cared enough to want to see us and let us know how he felt about Daddy," I said.

He stared into the bourbon and water he twisted back and forth in his hands.

"It's strange," he said.

Two mornings later, on my drive south to Montgomery, I thought that it wasn't strange at all.

I stared into my mother's ear. The more I stared, the more perfect it became: turning from a pale pink to a pristine white image.

She lay upon the high bed, suspended as though on a stage, her tiny head with high forehead reaching up into her sporadic hair that had become so delicate the white fibers could scarcely be combed together but rose separately and individually from her thin alabaster skull with tiny rivulets of blue and pink coursing just beneath the surface. The lights of the emergency room shone on her like stage-lights, dramatically full into her colorless face.

As I stared at the ear, it hardened, as though my staring was an action that caused it to transform itself into a crystal piece of art.

For a moment it seemed that her thin lips moved beneath the plastic oxygen mask, and I inched closer, put my hands upon her bony shoulders, and, in a frantic voice, I said, "Mama? You say something, Mama?"

I stared at her mouth that was drawn back against her teeth. She'd always had wonderful teeth. They had never stained. Unlike Daddy, she'd never smoked. Her teeth were hard and strong and white. But now they seemed too large for her mouth.

I gazed at her mouth, wanting, hoping, begging to hear something, a word, an utterance of last love, a blessing, something to take with me and to pass along, but the lips, now purple, were motionless.

The doctor moved behind me and the nurse beside him. He told me to say my goodbyes, and I lowered my head to her sallow cheek and kissed the cold skin. I rose away from her and touched the side of her head that had turned a brownish-yellow, and I wondered if something there had not killed her, but the doctor said it had been a combination of things: her aorta valve was half-closed and would not function properly. She was eighty-four and had had open-heart surgery that had not gone well four years earlier, and for the past few weeks she had been suffering a shortage of breath. Six months ago, she had to be rushed to the hospital from her home in Tuscaloosa. The doctors worked their magic, bringing her around, but since then her body had grown more and more frail with each passing day.

For the past five months, since the death of her second husband, my stepfather, a tough sturdy no-nonsense man of the earth, a man whose personality was as thick as his farm-raised, sun-baked skin, I had pleaded with her to come south a hundred miles to Montgomery to live near me. I had found an assisted-living facility populated mostly by elderly widows who kept each other company with planned meetings, discussion groups and Bible study devotionals. It was the kind of place Mama would like, I thought, now that she was confined to a wheelchair. It would beat the life she led at home: anchored to a Medicare chair all day to watch the monotonous grind of talk-show after talk-show on the never-quiet television, being lifted onto her potty-chair, and never ever experiencing the first semblance of conversation. Even her church visitors complained that when they came she sat and stared at the television, watching Oprah or Jenny or whomever, never even turning her head to listen to what they had to say. Her attention was fixed on the droning tv.

Finally, after Thanksgiving and Christmas and New Years, after I had described The Oaks as a paradise for senior citizens, after I said I simply could not continue to tromp up and down the highway, two hours north and two hours south, making the trip weekly and sometimes twice a week, that even my health at age fifty-nine could not hold to that pace, she turned to me one day and said, "Okay."

Just a simple one-word reply.

"What?" I asked, thinking that surely I had heard wrong.

"Okay," she said in her quiet stoic fashion.

So we made the plans. The grandsons brought her furniture. My wife hung pictures around the hand-carved mahogany bed. The granddaughters brought a Jeep Cherokee stacked with dresses and pantsuits, gowns and pajamas, hats and scarves and underwear, boxes crammed with costume jewelry, canisters of cosmetics.

A few days later, when she was wheeled into the room, after I brought her down in my six-year-old Lincoln which I'd had washed and vacuumed especially for the trip, she looked around and saw the photos of all of her children and grandchildren and great-grandchildren, and she smiled when she saw the small television set on the chest of drawers. She looked around for the remote control, which I had forgotten. I promised to fetch it immediately.

Regardless of circumstance, I was still her son, her little boy, willing and wanting to do her bidding. No matter age or place, she was mother, I son. And I rushed to provide her with the necessities to make her happy.

Reassuring herself that life would continue as before, she snapped the control buttons to flicker on Jerry Springer and his array of trailer park whores and pimps. On her first morning at the facility with its wide hallways, its windows open to banks of white and pink and red azaleas, she rolled down the hall and made an appointment to have her hair done and continued to the dining room where she obstinately pulled up to an empty table. Before a waitress could bring her breakfast, two of the blue-haired ladies from a nearby table stepped to her side, introduced themselves, and invited her to join them. She acquiesced.

Within minutes she was enjoying scrambled eggs, crisp bacon, toast and creamy grits with five other women, all of whom were widows between the ages of seventy-eight and eighty-nine. After listening to their various stories, each from small towns around Alabama, Myrtle Lee Hassell Morgan Adams began her tale. She told of losing her last husband, the proud welder from rural west Alabama, where he'd raised his own family before his wife died an untimely death nearly thirty years ago. She told of being married previously to a wild and unruly scoundrel, my father, whom she had also loved dearly and endured his literal craziness for more than two decades, before he finally succumbed to too many prescription drugs. She told of her grandchildren and their children, and twenty minutes later she gazed around exhausted at the alert, listening faces. She took a deep breath and let it out. She felt a pain in the depths of her sternum but thought nothing of it. She put her tiny fingers to the spot between her breasts that had been removed in a mastectomy more than thirty years ago. She smiled toothily and gasped, "I don't know when I've talked so much."

Her new friend, Alma Langham, a tall seventy-eight-year-old who lived only two doors down the hall pushed Mama's wheelchair. "We enjoy hearing you," Alma said, as she turned her over to Janice, the sitter who was waiting, watching television. Janice helped her into the Medicare chair, where she leaned back as far as it would go. With the television tuned to some innocuous show, she closed her eyes and was soon snoring softly.

That afternoon, Alma Langham rolled Mama to The Pub, a large brightly painted meeting room with round tables and pictures of funny-faced clowns on the wall. Attentively, Mama sat and listened to a middle-aged woman from the local Presbyterian church talk about Jesus and the apostles. She knew the stories well. She had taught a Sunday school class for senior citizens at the Baptist church she attended back home, when she had been able to go every week, before the illness had weakened her. But it had been a long time since she sat and listened and enjoyed the stories from the Bible. Her first husband had been Presbyterian and they had attended his church for a while when their sons were growing up. She saw little difference in the two religions. They were both Christian, and she believed deeply and strongly in Jesus Christ as her savior, and as far as she was concerned, that was that. Nothing else truly mattered. She had prayed long and hard, holding the hand of her second husband while cancer and the Lord took him away.

After the forty-minute devotional session, she once again felt the weight of something heavy pressing against her chest. Once again, she dismissed it as a sign of growing tired. She had not listened so intently to anything in a long while, and it made her both weary and happy.

At her room, Janice helped her into bed, where she lay on her back and closed her eyes and was asleep within moments. She dreamed about Jesus flying with her over a body of water. They floated together on a cloud. She felt cool but not cold. She was weightless, holding the gentle hand that guided her through the air. She had never liked heights, but she was not afraid.

She awakened with a smile.

I stood next to her bed and held her hand that was not half as large as mine. She gazed into my face, smiling.

"You've about worn yourself out, haven't you?" I asked.

She smiled. "Is it time for supper?" she asked.

The next afternoon the women of <u>The Oaks</u>, led by the social director, had a short story discussion in The Pub. The previous afternoon each had been given a large-print handout of "The Necklace" by Guy De Maupassant. When I noticed it on the table by her chair, I asked Mama if she'd read it. She gave a brief little nod.

"Is it the one about the couple borrowing the necklace to wear to a party?" I asked.

She nodded.

"Did they lose it?"

She nodded. She eyed me crossly, a scowl on her lips.

"What happened at the end?" I asked.

"I know what happened in the end," she said haughtily. "You're not going to catch me. They saved money through the years to pay for the necklace because they had returned a copy to the owner. Then they discovered the owner had originally given them only a fake. There is the twist." She smiled shrewdly. "There is the irony," she added.

I nodded and watched as Alma Langham pushed her down the hall toward their discussion group. I thought that it would be a good meeting. She certainly knew the story and understood it well.

Driving home, I recalled stories of Mama's childhood, traveling in a wagon across the South with her family, her father Bub Hassell an itinerant carpenter who had built a portable home in the vehicle pulled by a pair of matching mules. Granddaddy specialized in coffer-dams for power companies constructing hydroelectric plants. When he found a job he parked the wagon, folded out platforms to make beds on each side, unfolded a large V of canvas overhead, fitted together sectioned poles and fixed them into slots, raising them to make a tent to cover his family. In the wintertime it was too cold, in the summer too hot. They were generally kept dry in rainy weather except when the wind out of the northwest swirled counter-clockwise and lifted the canvas and dislodged the poles. When that happened, Myrtle and her brother lay quietly frightened in the darkness until Bub made it right. They learned early that their father did not abide whimpering or tears in the event of a natural disaster. Near the wagon he set up a cooking station protected by a tarpaulin where their mother, Emma McLean Hassell, a strong-shouldered Scotch-Irish, prepared their meals in her own silent but pleasant manner. Mama went to school in dozens of small towns in Georgia, Alabama, and Mississippi. In high school she learned French and read numerous books, including Victor Hugo's Les Miserables in the original language. Probably, I thought, De Maupassant's "The Necklace" was among the works she had studied back then. I wondered if she would tell the women about that experience, reading it in French under the light of a kerosene lamp and the moon.

The next morning I strode down the hallway of <u>The Oaks</u> with an excited gait. I wanted to ask her about the story and how the discussion went. I wondered if she knew other stories I had never heard about her traveling youth. But when I entered her room I saw immediately that the atmosphere had changed. Mama was lying in bed. Her face looked ashen. Janice mopped her brow with a damp rag.

After breakfast she'd gotten sick. Her stomach would not hold the food. For the past hour she had run a high fever.

I felt her brow.

It was clammy hot.

"Has she seen a doctor?" I asked.

Mama's eyes followed me as I moved toward Janice, who was running cold water over the rag. "The doctor saw her an hour ago and gave her some medicine," Janice said.

Later the doctor came back. After listening to her chest through the stethoscope, he said, "She needs to go to the hospital." He said I could take her in my car. Janice rolled her to the front door where I met them in my Lincoln. On the front seat, Mama said, "Why don't you clean your car, son?"

I didn't bother to answer that it was cleaner than it had been in months, especially for her.

At the hospital the uniformed attendants rushed her into the emergency room. I filled out the paperwork. Then I waited with Janice, seated with others who were waiting in front of television sets suspended from the ceiling.

By seven that night, after I had taken Janice home and she was replaced by Tommie Ann, another sitter, Mama was placed in a private room. They said her condition had stabilized.

Two hours later the cardiovascular physician, a tall handsome woman with coffee-and-cream complexion, entered the room with an air of authority. After introducing herself, she listened to Mama's heart. Moments later she showed me a drawing of a heart with a large hose opening from the bottom and two large pipes extending from the top. "These are the aorta valves," she said. "They are the chief arterial passageways that carry blood from the heart to be circulated throughout the body. The upper aorta carries blood to the brain. As you can see, if it is blocked, not enough blood is carried to the body and the brain."

"The body and brain die without circulation," I said.

I glanced toward Mama to see if I had spoken too loud.

She stared straight at the silent picture on the television screen, showing no sign of having heard my words.

The doctor, who had also glanced in her direction, nodded.

"Is there nothing you can do?" I asked.

"Treat her for the pneumonia, feed her oxygen, try to strengthen her, and hope she recovers enough to undergo physical rehabilitation."

The clear plastic tube attached around Mama's neck allowed oxygen to be breathed through her nose.

Time with her, for me, was a mixture of close moments, holding her tiny hand, combing my fingers through her stringy hair, looking down at her sharp nose with the plastic tube feeding enough oxygen to force her to live, and long minutes of pure desperation when I wanted to grab her and shake her and demand that she suck in the food of life and swallow grits-and-eggs. Live, dammit, live! I wanted to shout as she looked lifelessly at the television screen.

Four days later, after she had been treated with antibiotics dripping intravenously for hour after hour, after she had eaten only ice cream and high-calorie liquid sustenance, after she had lost the few pounds that had been clinging to her brittle bones, and after she had spoken only monosyllables and could not be engaged in conversation concerning de Maupassant's "The Necklace," much less her childhood, she was taken to the rehabilitation center next door to The Oaks. There I again did the paperwork and her doctor ordered the oxygen continued. For three days she lay in the bed with a therapist visiting daily, gingerly lifting her broom-handle legs and stick-like arms. Each time he lifted, she winced. She gazed at me with a deep hurt in her watery eyes. I lowered my face over hers and kissed her forehead and her cheeks. I said, "I love you," and she mouthed the same words.

On the fourth morning when I entered she was gasping for breath. Tommie Ann had already called the nurse. "She started just a few minutes ago," Tommie Ann explained, standing back with me against the wall as we watched the nurse check her pulse and listen for a heartbeat.

Straightening, the nurse said, "I've called an ambulance," the edge of panic in her voice.

When I said, "Mama," she stared straight into my eyes. As I followed behind the ambulance, I still pictured her glassy eyes staring into mine. I knew that she was looking deeper than she had ever looked. She saw inside me: into the background, even before my memory: the beginning, when she married my father in the first store-bought dress she'd ever owned; the middle, with a wild man who died quietly in the middle of the night when he was only fifty-three and she was fifty, and later, with a good strong hardy country man who was short on excitement but fulfilling and unrelenting in his love for her, and . . . I tried to picture a scene from the past but it all came apart, blurry and unfocused. I saw only her eyes: big gray-green frightened eyes.

After we waited below the television sets for a half-hour the doctor came out and motioned for me. I went to her. Silently, her arm circled my back and pressed there, guiding me through an automatic door. We wove between a half-dozen other doctors and nurses, all concerned with their various duties. At another door, she said, "She has only a short while. Go in and say good-bye. Her heart's just worn out."

I closed my eyes and opened them quickly. I stepped through the doorway into the room where Mama was suspended in the bed, lights on her, spotlighting her final moments.

The next time I saw her ear it was resting next to the soft white silk cushion of the coffin. It had turned to pure crystal as though shaped by a master artist's hands, twisted and turned and smoothed. It was the closest thing to perfection I had ever seen, and soon I would see it no longer.

The singer sang, "Amazing Grace," her fine voice cracking on a high note, the sound lingering long after the faceless preacher said his meaningless words. We filed out behind the silver gray box draped in pink-and-white roses and funeral ferns dotted with delicate little white buds.

I tried, but my mind could never again form the perfect shape of Mama's ear as it had existed only a few moments earlier.

A c k n o w l e d g m e n t s

All books are collaborations. No matter how strongly a writer might feel that every morning he is crawling within himself and writing in pure isolation, he is truly writing about all of those people and all of those experiences that have contributed to his work and to his life. I learned long ago that I am in debt to all of those who inhabit my world and who enrich it in spite of my own personal stubborn ignorance.

I could not possibly thank all of the people who influenced and helped make up these stories. People who have known me throughout the years of their making will imagine they know who certain characters are. They are wrong. While I have lived the essence of the title story when I was a boy, the dream itself is a world of wonder, as it is with the stories that follow.

The folks at River City Publishing are greatly appreciated in the finishing of this work that has been long in the making. And I want thank my friends at 1048 Blues & Jazz Club: Adrian, Fran, Tangela, Bart, Warren, Clay, Dave P, John, Jon, George, Will, Donovan, Knox, Rhodes, and Doug, all of whom have given much to add a flavor to this old life.

My family contributed much to these stories. But it is not about them. It is not autobiography. And yet the fabric of life that I lived with wonderful people gave these stories a texture they would not otherwise have. My mother and father and brother are gone now. I see much of them in my nieces and nephew: Donna, Anna, Krysten, and Daren.

I have had so many wonderful teachers throughout my life. If I have any success in developing my dream, it is their doing. There was the old master, Hudson Strode at the University of Alabama, who proclaimed that all of his students were successes simply by being allowed to study under his guidance. My old friends, Borden Deal and Babs H. Deal, showed the student what it meant to work hard and be true to his art. James Jones bought a beer on a hot afternoon and offered no advice. Margaret Cousins, a great editor at Doubleday, pointed me south toward home. Tay Hohoff, another great editor at J.B. Lippincott, preached, "Rewrite! Rewrite! Rewrite!" And my lovely friend Nelle Harper Lee suggested I put these experiences together into a collection.

My gracious wife, Sally, is the best teacher of all because she is gentle with her criticism and allows me the freedom to find my way out of the wilderness. She is my best and most beautiful critic.

Wayne Greenhaw
Montgomery, Alabama